Stones in the River

Stones in the River

20 award-winning short stories

by Jim Koenig

Stones in the River: 20 Award-Winning Short Stories

ISBN: 978-0-578-70951-2

Cover photograph: Shenandoah River at Harpers Ferry by Susanne Koenig
Interior Artwork by Susanne Koenig
Book Design by Catherine Baldau

To the three in my life most beloved and admired,
Adriane,
Emily,
and Susanne

Contents

Introduction

Time travel,
Travel back in time,
Time to tidy things up,
Things don't change,
Change happens all the time,
Time to get to work.

I've fiddled long enough with assembling a collection of my short stories, so at long last, finally here it is. Now that I am 70, the notion has become more insistent that I should leave something for posterity, something that shouts, "I was here!"

Though it's an arduous slog to write stories, once they're done it should be easy enough to stack them in a neat pile, add a title and fancy it up with cover art. Easy because, years ago the annual West Virginia Writers Contest periodically offered a category for judging collections as yet unpublished. I submitted to this category a few different times: in 1993 (I won a third-place award), in 1997 (honorable mention), and 2001 (first place, plus a first place for another short story submission). While not a quick writer, I am persistent and had produced enough material to compile these initial short story collections. So why was I coming up against such a barrier when it came to assembling my collection 'for real?'

What was different this time?

My usual pace hadn't changed. I was still winning an award or publishing a story about every other year. The obvious answer is, I had changed. I began to think about why I wrote at all.

I had been writing story after story, yet it turned out that it was without a clear sense of why I felt the need to write. In the process of compiling my stories for this collection, I was revisiting them as a whole and, as I began to read them critically a realization slowly dawned on me. Writing hadn't been just a way to spend the early morning hours on the weekends as I had done for more than three decades. I had used my writing as a form of therapy, as my wife and editor had understood all along: "You're writing unconsciously from your subconscious," she once said.

That became obvious even to me once I began reading each story anew and encountering associations with my early memories. That really slowed me down. I got to the point where I'd go months at a time without working on the collection. I even committed with single-minded devotion to the demanding challenge of expanding an award-winning story into a short story trilogy. It proved to be a very effective way to avoid working on the collection.

In my thirties, seemingly out of the blue, I developed an urge to write short stories. Up to that point I'd had no experience or interest in writing fiction. This came at a transitional time in my personal relationships and career when the future held excitement and promise. What I didn't realize then was that my childhood was quietly beckoning me to attend to a lot of deferred mourning. Without knowing it, writing became my way of working through that process. Ideas came at random, gifts from a benevolent Story Muse. But in retrospect, it seems as if many were unknowingly dredged up from a well of hurt and sadness.

There were plenty of signs that this was the case had I been paying attention. My first story to gain public recognition, *Maiden Flight, Be Mine,* contained themes from my childhood that would be addressed in one way or another in most of the stories that followed. Looking back, my upbringing seems more notable for an absence of oversight than any diligent maternal or paternal attention. At the time (and probably not singular to my neighborhood), there were legions of us. Boys like me were "free range" before there was a name for such a thing, with one or both parents absent because of working two and three jobs yet still never enough money, or just worn out trying to take care of a large family. Then there was a far too familiar overuse of alcohol. In my case, it was all of the above.

Kids like me did what we could to survive mostly by taking care of ourselves and earning some money of our own, maybe delivering newspapers until we turned sixteen when we could get a work permit for a better paying night job pumping gas or stocking shelves. We went to public high schools but dropped out at alarming rates while waiting impatiently to turn eighteen so we could get into a union apprenticeship. Those that landed good paying jobs invariably bought a new car, soon got married, and began having kids of their own.

What I now see in my stories wasn't evident or intentional while I was writing them. But a feeling of aloneness permeates them—any sympathetic view of motherhood is absent, fathers are inept though usually well meaning, death often hovers in the wings if not front and center. The disintegration of a family or relationships seems inevitable. What keeps these stories from being altogether depressing is that each protagonist senses or gains a conviction that things might get better. In the final paragraph of *Alone in the Galaxy*, a young boy finds refuge in an old Ford Galaxie 500, a car once to be envied but now nothing but an abandoned wreck. Even as he contemplates desolation, he envisions a scenario that fairly crackles with a sense of freedom:

> "I gripped the steering wheel and imagined the car brand new, the radio playing, all the gauges flickering, and the big V-8 pounding under the hood. I'm sixteen, maybe seventeen, barreling down the highway, the speedometer dead on seventy with the music cranked-up higher than the wind and, for a little while, I don't feel alone."

As a child I, too, longed for things to get better. But they only tended to get worse and, of necessity, I became mostly self-sufficient, coming and going to school or work seemingly unnoticed by my parents. However, like the protagonists in my stories, I could somehow see beyond the mess of the then present to a future that offered promise, however tenuous.

I wasn't aware of this as a theme until I asked my daughter, Adriane, to read one of my stories. "Wistful," was her judgment and my wife reinforced this adding, "All of your stories are wistful," as if that would be obvious to anyone reading them, let alone to the person who conceived them.

What I've come to recognize after thirty plus years of writing stories is that I unwittingly gave voice to that inner child who longed just once to be patted on the shoulder and have his father or teacher say, "You're a bright boy!" This bashful child must have flashed a sly grin after each story that earned an award or was actually published because someone had finally noticed what he had ever yearned to prove.

All of the stories in this collection have won an award and/or have been published. Not one of them would have been possible without

3

the patient support and editorial help from my wife, Susanne, who recognized better than anyone the bright boy within that fathered the man who wrote these.

Interlude

My old man, Rosser, wasn't in our crappy motel room. On the way back I'd rattled the door at the VFW and it had just closed. He was on foot. It was turning cold and I had the trench coat he'd left behind.

I wore my surplus army jacket with a Day-Glo orange peace symbol painted on the back. Instead of carrying his coat, I squeezed it on over my own. It was like putting on his skin because of the booze and cigarette stink. A quick pat located his pint and smokes and in the other pocket was his buckeye. It was a country boy thing, an Ohio lucky charm, a fat glossy brown nut that you couldn't even eat.

When loaded, Rosser fixed a Camel between his index and middle fingers while absently rolling and rubbing a buckeye in his other hand, waiting for Lady Luck to walk in a tavern and wink at him. Instead, some woozy old broad would sidle-up and cadge a couple of drafts and half a dozen smokes before taking him home. Probably didn't happen tonight because he's been pissed-off about something and guzzled more than usual. I just about got loaded myself before that groovy chick pulled me away to dance and I lost track of my old man.

While searching for him I found two bars still open with a few Rosser look-alikes—wiry old men with G.I. flattops and closely-shaved red faces hunched over shots and sweaty mugs. They eyeballed me for a millisecond while stubbing out butts in crowded, smoldering ash-trays. I could tell by the way they looked at me they thought I was a draft dodger. That's what World War II vets like Rosser thought about hippies.

He wasn't in the bar, so I hit the road out to Memorial Park. Once beyond the reach of streetlights, a bright moon spooked up the land-scape as I pushed deeper into the night. Fucking Rosser, what a trip!

Stopping at the park entrance I could hear faint grunting noises. I tracked the sounds, my eyes stopping at the cluster of war memori-als. Something or someone seemed to be hugging the puny Vietnam monument put up by the town in the early days of the war when the first casket arrived containing a local boy and everybody knew there'd eventually be more. Town talk was right on: it did look like a fat park-ing lot bollard with a tilted brass hat. A compromise, they said. Most Viet vets wanted to forget while the senior set remembered long ago wars, worthy of grand monuments.

A heroic granite monolith loomed nearby unmolested. WWI claimed one massive face and WWII the other, scores of homeboy names chiseled in neat soldierly rows: KIA's move column right, survi-vors move column left; all heroes to the home folks.

A third memorial displayed a weary life-size bronze dogface crouching atop a high pedestal. An alert soldier trapped forever in the cold hilly landscape listened intently for the enemy in northeast Korea near the Chosin Reservoir. Soon, waves of Red Chinese would make his life a freezing hell, a brave soldier even in retreat.

From about ten feet away I began to make out a man on his knees, arms wrapped around the stubby concrete pillar topped with a plaque that honored Viet vets. Whatever the hell he was doing sure looked like he was trying to rock the stunted monument out of the ground. This was kooky and just like Rosser when he was really polluted. I sat down on a park bench.

The bollard had won that round when the scrawny old man re-leased his hold and settled back on his heels. It was my father, all right. There were black splotches on Rosser's moonlit face and hands that were either dirt or blood. His clothes were a mess.

He didn't seem surprised to find me watching.

6

"Looks like you could use some help," I said, although he never wanted any from his disappointment-of-a-son, recent college dropout and in his mind, a soon-to-be draft dodger.

Rosser's breath came in short gasps. "You can give me a goddamn smoke," he huffed, struggling to his feet. Finding his legs, he wobbled over and sat down heavily on the far side of the bench.

I fished out the pack and pint and set them down between us. A small flame wavered underneath the cigarette, his hand unsteady. A long pull off the bottle followed.

"Don't be stupid," he said at last. "We had the damn war won," he spoke in the same ruined rummy's voice that seemed to always need a great hacking cough to clear.

I figured he was talking about his war, WWII, but it could be now. The Viet Cong were whipped, the crew cut spit-shined generals told the president, congress, and us. Then came the Tet Offensive and all the war protestors poured onto the streets. I had their look—beard, beads and long hair—because it was the thing to do, but until now the war had been somebody else's problem. Then I lost my deferment and got my draft notice.

"We'd be home for Christmas," Rosser continued. "Hell, we didn't even have winter gear. Then came the Bulge." He took another long pull then put the bottle down on the bench between us.

I expected he'd walk away, probably sobered up just enough to be embarrassed since he never talked about the War.

"Keep the fuckin' buckeye," Rosser hissed, "and don't believe army bullshit, ever." He got up and wobbled back to the small monument and knelt down hard against it. Locking his arms around the Vietnam memorial, he grunted and rocked trying to rip it from the earth.

Bathed in lunar light, I sipped the dregs of whiskey and watched him do his thing. Was it his war or my soon-to-be war that was making him nuts?

After a couple of minutes, I shed his trench coat and tossed it on the bench. My surplus army jacket reminded me that my draft number was up and, in a week, I had to report to Fort Holibird for my induction physical.

Shoving his shiny buckeye into my back pocket, I marched over to help whether he wanted any or not.

The end.

Love 1968

Crap, is all I can think. In the distance, squiggles of smoke rise from the Baltimore skyline. *Crap and crap.* It's got so I can hardly make it through the week just to get to my crappy part-time job pushing a broom, unpacking boxes and stocking shelves. *Crap on a cheese cracker times three.* What if she's not even working today with all the rioting downtown and on top of that it's Easter Sunday?

I don't have a car, so I've got to walk to my job at the drugstore. Edmondson Avenue is so empty it's creepy, like a nuclear war is about to start and everybody's gone to a bomb shelter. Nobody's going to church or having Easter egg hunts even though this morning there's hardly any smoke over the ghettos. The Negroes are probably tired of rioting and, just my luck, school will open back up tomorrow.

Crap on a creepy customer. I've got all these crazy "crap" sayings in my head 'cause my dad has a ton of them. He says it instead of that other word, 'cause he's not supposed to cuss in front of us kids.

9:55 a.m., April 7, 1968 – the fuzzy blue ink stamps the Sunday slot on my time card. The jitters start the second I punch in. I'm in love for the first time and everything I'd rehearsed to say just went blank like when I take a math test. *Shit!* I yell inside my head, knowing that if an adult or girl were around and heard me, I'd be in trouble. Someday I'll be on my own and can yell anything I want.

"Here," Dr. Goldberg says scaring the heck out of me. He's holding out a canvas deposit bag. "Take this up front then go downstairs and unpack the shipment."

"Yessir," I answer. 'Up front' is the checkout counter where she should be standing, just like the past eight Sundays. From that very first day I can't get over those deep brown eyes. If she smiles or talks to me, I'm so nervous around her I almost get sick.

I grab a push broom and go to the plate glass window. In the distance, the smoke on the Baltimore skyline rises like spirals from our living room ashtrays. The six o'clock news has been full of bug-eyed Negroes pumping their fists and screaming, "Burn baby, burn!" To me the city skyline doesn't look too much worse. There's always a fire or two somewhere. *Crap on a coconut cookie.*

I sneak a sideways glance then bite my tongue, *What?*

I know it's got to be her but behind the counter toting up the cash register seems like some different girl entirely. Instead of her hair pulled back in a kind of "twist," I guess they call it, it's puffed out in Afro style. I'm used to seeing her in a plaid skirt and white shirt she's been wearing to work, but today's she's in a hippie outfit. 'My' Janet wears a little nice makeup even with skin so smooth she doesn't need it, and without any I know I'd still be in love. I've thought about what to say if someone commented on it.

"It's like dark caramel," I'd say then laugh, "ha, ha . . . a lot of summer sun from tennis camp!"

Creeping toward her I sneak the bag onto the counter and slip away. She'd have to be blind not to see my arm shaking. Her head bobs with each bill placed on a stack. "Thanks," she says and continues, ". . . five, six, seven . . ." not looking up at me.

Run, baby, run, pops into my head and I have to screw my mouth shut to keep from busting out. Ducking behind the row with the crappy Easter stuff and sucking wind, I sneak a peek over the top like a Marine in the Mekong Delta.

Geez, I'm so in love.

"Jimmy," yells Dr. Goldberg, scaring the pants off me again. "Daydream downstairs while you unpack the shipment."

"Yessir," I answer but keep pointing my head like a bird dog. From this far away I think of things I could have said, "I really like your new hair style," or, "You look great." But I'm not one of the cool guys at Woodlawn High with a Mustang and the Joe College looks.

* * *

I take all day to unpack and sort the shipment of summer goods like folding chairs, inflatable rafts, cases of Coppertone and crap like that—stuff I'd never buy because we don't go to Ocean City. My family's such a bunch of losers.

Dr. Goldberg didn't check on me. I guess he's got riots on the brain, like my dad who says over-and-over, "What do those Negroes want anyway?" and, "If they move any closer to us, we're moving." That means to West Virginia, where he bought a quarter acre near Harpers Ferry. He just might do it this time because God knows he loves dragging us out to the woods every summer instead of to the shore at Ocean City.

This is what really scares me. Dad packing us off to the sticks and never seeing Janet again. I'd have to run away or die. *Crap on country camping.*

* * *

It's getting late, and I hustle to sweep the store and empty trash. Pushing my broom toward the front, I keep my head down hoping to blow past the checkout counter unnoticed. Janet's voice stops me like a brick wall, "Hey, are you mad at me or something?" Her voice is as smooth as her dark skin.

Making like a statue, I don't want to look at her because I'm already too nervous. But I say, "Why?" and loosen up a little making fake sweeping motions.

"You haven't said 'boo' to me all day," she says like we're friends, "and I was just wondering."

She's to blame with her militant get up, no lipstick or nail polish and a frizzy Afro like that Commie sick-o professor Angela Davis. But I kind of mumble, "Dr. Goldberg," while jerking my head toward the pharmacy counter. My face is on fire because I'm a total sap in love.

I take two steps then some space alien takes hold and I actually turn to look and she's smiling. My legs wobble but the alien kidnaps my brain and uses my voice to say, "I'm sorry." I lean on my broom to steady myself. Pinned to her shirt pocket is a badge showing Martin

10

Luther King, Jr. with his thin little moustache. Around the border I read, THE DREAM IS ALIVE!"

I want to run outside with my broom but even though she's not the same Janet I fell in love with I can't stop looking at her.

"That's okay, Jimmy," she says so nicely. "I guess things are a little crazy."

"Yeah," I say back, but it sounds too happy and I lower my voice and say, "I know what you mean." I really don't. Pinned to her other pocket is a small, orange badge with a Black Power fist. Now she's going to think I'm staring at her boobs like some drooling kid, so I say too loudly, "I better sweep outside."

I bust through the double front doors dragging the broom behind me.

Except for the burning stink from blocks away, the warm spring air is great because Janet talked to me. I'm in love again. She cared that I haven't talked to her in a week or two.

Nobody's been around. Everyone is laying low. The white people are pretty scared and angry. The Negroes are just angry. So there's not too much crap to sweep and then I can go back inside and see her again and maybe even have a real conversation. But wait, did she mean it was "okay" I hadn't said a word because I was busy or because she thinks I'm bummed out about Dr. King getting shot? What would impress her most?

"Jimmy!"

Crap on a cockeyed cockroach.

A guy can't even think for a minute. Not twenty feet away are three of the coolest kids at Woodlawn. Of course I know their names, everybody does, but they'd never talk to me so they must want something.

"Jimmy, my man!" Mark hoots, waving for me to come over.

I sweep slowly but can't think of what they might want. They already have cool clothes, nice cars, and don't have to work. Maybe they want me to crawl to show I know how cool they are?

Crap on a crooked crutch.

"What's happenin', my oppressed working-class brother?" Mark jives but doesn't high five for some skin. Probably thinks I'm swarming with cooties. Donna, his beautiful girlfriend, stands beside him. Next to her is Crazy Bob. He gets into fights all the time and looks ready to slug somebody.

"Tell me, mah soul brother, whuh's happenin' on this *faaahn* Sunday?" Mark says, trying to sound like a Negro.

11

I know he's mocking how some of them talk.

Play along, I tell myself and say, "Not much," and shrug. I'll bet he's never even been alone in the same room with a black person.

"Not riotin' with the people?" Mark jives, sounding even more stupid. Nodding toward Crazy Bob, he says, "He primed to kick some butt for his people."

Crazy Bob rips the cellophane off a new pack of Marlboros and drops it on the ground at my feet. After tapping the box on the heel of his hand, he slowly lights a cigarette and inhales just like the cowboy on TV. The matchbook has the drugstore name on the cover.

Shaking out the match, Crazy Bob smiles his evil smile then takes another deep drag while studying me like a bug he's about to squash. Instead, he drops the dead match at his feet next to the cellophane wrapper. I resist the urge to say, "Hey, I've got to clean up this crap!"

But a light bulb pops on. *With almost everything being closed, they've stopped just to bust on me because they've got nothing else to do. At school I'm just one of hundreds of nobodies but here they'll rip me just because I'm alone and they know I won't do a thing about it.*

Like he's Steve McQueen, Crazy Bob squints at the empty four-lane highway that runs straight downtown. Usually there are lots of cars whizzing by. With her fine silky blonde hair tucked behind each ear, Donna stands like a Breck Shampoo girl. Everybody knows, if he wants, Mark can go all the way with any girl. I'd give anything just to do it one time. Then maybe I could tell someone at school and guys would punch me in the shoulder and smile like I've joined the club.

The three of them look at me and I finally say, "What am I doing? Nothing. Just hanging loose."

"Power to the people!" Mark yells and raises a fist in the black power salute.

I realize I'm supposed to answer and shout, "Right on, brother!" I laugh and think maybe there's no harm in making a little fun of Negroes. I mean, who does it hurt?

Mark then makes his hand into a pistol and points it at me. He looks like a TV detective about to grill a suspect. "Hey, bro, what do you really think about Negroes?"

Crap on a copycat.

Janet's face is suddenly in my head. My face flames hotter than a burning building. Christ, I might as well have "I love Negroes" painted on my greasy forehead. Don't they see she could easily be any senior with a nice beach tan? But there aren't any militant Negroes at Woodlawn High, just an old janitor and a couple of fat cafeteria ladies.

Crap on Crispy Critters, the one and only cereal that comes in the shape of animals.

"What do you mean?" I ask, hoping they're pulling my leg. But I already know. With Negroes looting and burning, everybody seems to be taking sides.

Crazy Bob walks slowly behind me, then says in his tough guy deep voice, "Answer the frigging question." I imagine he's still squinting at the empty highway.

The burning stink suddenly makes my mouth dry and I cough real loud to work up a juicy hocker, but no luck. Thinking fast and praying they're just messing around, I answer, "They're okay, but I wouldn't want one to marry my sister."

Then I laugh like a mental case, "Haw, haw, haw." My guts are shaking.

Crap on cold concrete, which I just might in a minute.

Mark clicks his tongue like a teacher when I give a stupid answer. He says to Crazy Bob, "You gonna take that?"

Quickly I start to say, "I got to get back," but don't finish as Bob's fist drives into my kidney. "*Huuaah*," flies out of my mouth along with all my breath.

"Crazy Bob's mother's a Nigger!" shouts Mark.

I'm out of it, but I hear Donna squeal, "Mark, that's not nice!"

Crap on crappy conversations.

Gripping my knees, I can't help a little laugh. Crazy Bob has blonde hair, blue eyes and his mother is probably head of the Junior League and his father president of the Board of Hunting Hills Country Club.

When I catch my breath, Crazy Bob is standing toe-to-toe with me. He blows cigarette smoke in my face, and says, "Tell that Nigger she don't belong here." He nods toward the front door, almost bumping my head.

Quickly, I back up two big steps and say, "I got to get working." I've never fought anyone, not even for a girl.

"Jimmy, my main man," Mark says, no longer funny. "I wouldn't let Crazy Bob marry my sister, either." Then he looks toward downtown and says, "The brothers are restless today."

More squiggles fill the skyline, some real close, closer than they've been, probably Edmondson Village. Dad's likely packing the car with food, water, blankets and his old army pistol from World War II. *Crap on campfire cooking.*

Mark clears his throat and I look at him. He'll go to Harvard or someplace like that, get a job making plenty of dough and marry a fashion model. If I'm lucky, I'll get a union job at Sparrows Point and marry one of those chubby girls with a zit face and lots of blue eye shadow.

Mark holds out his hand to shake. "No hard feelings."

My slimy hand takes his, cool-as-a-cucumber, and for the first time I smell his cologne. *All my men wear English Leather or nothing at all*, I think of the ad in *Playboy* and stupidly say, "Guess I'll see you at school."

"Come on, kids," Mark says, and they follow him across the parking lot to a Mustang convertible. The big engine roars to life and the Beatles begin blasting from an eight-track tape player. I hear John scream, "You say you want a revolution." Donna looks straight ahead but twiddles her fingers at me as the car barrels west away from the burning city.

While I take a hard look at downtown, a big shiny Buick pulls up. Janet flies out of the store and hops in. I can just see that she scoots across the seat and quickly kisses the driver. *Her father*, I guess—I hope—because no teenager would drive an old folk's car.

The tires smoke and squeal as the Buick makes a wicked U-turn and races toward downtown. *Crap on this crummy country.*

Now I have to worry for another whole week.

The end.

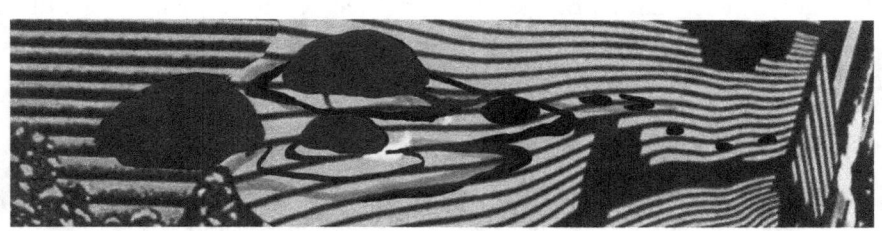

Things Most Surely Believed Among Us

"You look interesting," she said, coming to a halt amid the milling crowd. "I'd like at least one last intelligent conversation before the computers crash and we descend into chaos," she laughed. "You're the writer, aren't you?"

Mangling my collarbone with his grip, just then Jolly Ted clamps down on my shoulder with his ham hand. "See you've met Stuart our resident wordmeister," he greets the lovely woman I only just this moment laid eyes on.

"Written anything lately," he was asking me, but his rosy flushed, gray-whiskered face smiled for the woman. I secretly wished him a massive coronary and, in a split-second out of time, made a bold decision.

"*The New Yorker* is interested in one of my stories"—quite an imaginative stretch on such a spur of the moment—but then one of my resolutions for the new year, if we were all still here unscathed, was to start writing again.

Tonight the Anderson's castle shone as bright and cheery as a Christmas tree. The Andersons had recruited me to write the community association newsletter, hence my ticket to this evening's grand New Year's send-off, saying farewell to 1999 and welcoming in a brand-new millennium. Ted Anderson, big-time entrepreneur, and Naomi the much younger, gorgeous and quite talented potter, were the effervescent, all-inclusive hosts of the evening.

"Kristyn's got quite a story herself," Ted said, ignoring me except for the forgotten catcher-sized mitt compressing my sagging shoulder. His other beefy hand strangled the long neck of a Sam Adams. "But I guess you know that."

Kristyn demurred, a delicate manicured hand raised in dismissal. The beast gave my shoulder another vicious squeeze before letting go and, taking Kristyn by the elbow, said, "We need to talk," and to me, "*Ciao* for now." No bucking this slick maneuver, Kristyn tossed an exasperated look my direction. Melding into the crush Ted shouted back, "… catch you later about joining the Historic District Committee. …" Kristyn glanced back once again before they disappeared into the tide of well dressed, beautifully coiffed guests.

While the old millennium's hourglass emptied, the minutes ticking away, shouldn't I be poised beside an ATM somewhere as it starts spewing greenbacks onto the sidewalk like parade confetti? Or at 12:01 a.m. Saturday morning, January 1, 2000, would ATM access vaporize and leave the world cashless? Could two critically absent digits confuse the computers into calculating that 2000 was 1900 and actually start crashing airplanes, erase bank accounts, or leave all the stoplights dark in New York City? Booming drunken voices and belly laughs erupted randomly. A din of golden oldies seeped from some distant recess and swirled in the air like smoke at a pot party.

Wishing I hadn't worn these khakis with the ink stain on the left leg and this plain white shirt, I puzzled over what had possibly prompted me to depart the warmth of my 14-year-old Honda Civic to come on in. I had watched in wonder as a couple dressed to the nines in tailored suits slid like quicksilver up the front steps and, for a moment, bright lights and music poured from the open door before closing again. Ordinarily the last thing I wanted to do was shoot the breeze with this bunch wringing their hands over emergent crabgrass, SUV gas mileage, or Junior's SAT scores. Here was I, a Y2K paranoid, agonizing for the past few months trying to decide if computers really might go haywire and whether I should be outfitting a bunker for the chaos that would undoubtedly follow.

Was chaos really coming? In the months leading up to the new millennium, that was the big question on everybody's mind. To me, the bigger question was, *What should I do about it?*

I thought once again of the 20-gallon plastic buckets of survival food, nutrient dense, I should have purchased. I'd sat on the fence dithering about the purchase, my usual indecisive recourse in the face of life's dilemmas.

Like so many, I was both excited and apprehensive this New Year's Eve 1999. As I had sat in my car gazing at the Anderson's dazzling manse, I couldn't let go of the worry. Shouldn't I go home, fill up water jugs, pack snacks, grab a couple of books and hide in the basement with a candle and flashlight with fresh batteries? Who would want to hear about the world as-we-know-it melting down, which was all that was on my mind?

Clusters of well-heeled festive neighbors made their way up to the Anderson's turret-topped Victorian seemingly without a care in the world. I had an engraved invitation, was freshly scrubbed and dressed in my fashion clueless Sunday best. Suddenly, contrary to my nature, I wanted to be drunk on friendship and good feelings and leap into the New Year come-what-may, believing that things would be better.

Time to go in and mingle.

Heightened anticipation saturated the air and made even a teetotaler like me woozy with excitement. My Ex believed I didn't make friends. What did she know? Witness I was primed to chuck the old and lustily embrace the new with the best of middle-class America lucky enough to live in or near Hunt Country Estates. Admittedly, it took some effort to put on this persona but, for a change, at least I was trying.

The house was chockablock full of adults littering the place and knee-high kids tearing after each other. Some heads turned and vaguely nodded to me though no one made any welcoming overtures. But the hubbub was as pleasant as a babbling brook, for the moment anyway.

The gregarious Andersons were not really my friends, as in *real* friends. They and the other Estatees were newer transplants, most who commuted to the city for work. Like Columbus, I got here first (after my divorce) and bought a modest old farmhouse a few years before real estate prices shot out of sight and the farmland got sliced into estate-sized lots. That was how I was able to afford 'membership' on just a modest paying job as freelance editor of technical manuals (though, to confess, I can't even tackle programming a VCR). In the meantime, I've managed to get a few but unremarkable short stories published.

Not to mention penning the aforesaid Association Newsletter.

Anything was possible I wanted to believe at least tonight, that is until Jolly Ted just whisked away my prize find of the evening. While the millennium's hourglass emptied, I dawdled hopefully and was finally rewarded. To wit, the lovely and talented Naomi Anderson, wife of possibly trysting Ted entered the room, chin high, striding with purpose and trailing the most gorgeous mane of styled blond locks imaginable. She looked like Farrah Fawcett, golden and windblown. I felt immediately better.

"Thrown any pots lately?" I said, scrambling to snag her. A prize catch she would be for any man.

Naomi turned and smiled faintly, absently hooking a skein of flaxen hair behind a delectable ear.

"James!" she brightened visibly with overplayed delight and flung her arms around my neck. "Happy New Year," she whispered sweetly in my ear, obviously confused, high as a kite, bonkers, lonely or e) all of the above. We clung to each other and wobbled in a kind of slow dance like Kate and Leonardo on the deck of the Titanic.

Just go with it, I decided. Kristyn was probably occupied elsewhere or would come to her senses and turn to someone genuinely interesting for that final intelligent conversation.

No sooner had I rested my chin on Naomi's shoulder and whiffed the earthy smell of her golden locks then I spotted a bedrock Estatee groping someone-not-his-wife in a darkened nook. A calculation took over.

With all the grace of a 12-year-old boy retreating from his maiden aunt, I unstuck myself. Mumbling was what I did in these situations— something like, "Uh, thanks." Naomi, on the other hand, brightly wished me much happiness before spinning on her spiked heels and sashaying away, bent on maximum mingling like the good hostess.

In the hour remaining before midnight I sampled conversations and, like a mooning teenager, quietly searched hoping I still might find Kristyn. Anxiously roaming, I fervently hoped for a midnight kiss with her if Ted, the fat glutton, hadn't gobbled her up. Nudging around clusters of revelers, I smiled and scanned faces, but no luck.

Over-peopled now, I decided to be alone for a bit before midnight struck.

The last stop on my self-guided tour of the rambling house was the ascent up a hexagonal tower, the pride of Victorian architecture. Isn't it a universal rule that the third floor is off limits except for royalty? Aware that midnight was fast approaching, I crept like a cat burglar in Windsor Castle. The tower room was semi-dark, but I was drawn in by the view it afforded. Below, beyond the vast backyard deck and manicured lawn, Hunt Country Estates twinkled with elaborately competitive Christmas light displays.

"Stuart?" A tentative voice startled me. What had I walked in on?

"It's the writer!" Kristyn said happily. In the dim light, she lounged on a tufted leather davenport. She seemed comfortably ensconced in this walnut paneled room worthy of *Architectural Digest*.

The spout of an empty magnum of champagne nuzzled her shapely thigh, sculpted no doubt at Gold's Gym by many gray, sweaty hours before sunrise. Patting the bloated cushion next to her in invitation, she startled me by the sober clarity of her eyes.

I hesitated. Hadn't I come up here to be alone? I started to turn away and excuse myself.

"I don't bite," she said, "though I am *famished*." Her eyes had a faint glow in their depths.

What made me stay, I don't know? This ivory tower would definitely offer the perfect viewpoint to watch the world plunge into dark mayhem as the electrical grid crashed on the stroke of midnight.

I shrugged and sat uneasily on what was probably Ted's casting couch. No matter. Tonight, I'd settle for being just a nosh to tide her over until she got to her next engagement.

"All alone?" I asked, though I really didn't want an answer.

"Not anymore," she said sounding pleased. I felt better even if she was playing with me.

"I'm not really a writer as in *real* writer," I confessed, feeling compelled to lay my cards on the table, "Though I am known for my witty and captivating newsletters."

"Well, everybody in this 'burb wants to think you are," she said cheerily. "It makes them feel more glamorous and important, I guess, knowing *a writer*. But that's their hang up." Her eyes widened to emphasize her sincerity.

In my heart of hearts I ached to be a writer, but was more likely to build a short-wave radio from table scraps before I would scribble a prize-winning story.

"If wanting were doing, Oprah would have called by now," I said, admitting the truth I hadn't even fully acknowledged to myself.

As I was confiding this, she picked up the bottle that had been so contentedly nestled by her side, squinted at the label a moment and let it drop to the thick pile carpet with a dull thud.

"Was it good?" I asked, then realized she might be savoring her shenanigans with evil Ted. "The champagne," I quickly added.

"Somebody else killed that soldier. Scouts honor," she smiled, holding up three fingers in pledge.

Go. No-go. Gas pedal to the floor or jam on the brake?

I floored it. "What does everybody say about you?"

Her lovely face clouded, and I didn't know why.

"How long have you lived here?"

"Six years, why?"

"It's a sure bet you don't get out much, do you?"

I pled guilty.

"What got you out from under your rock tonight?"

"The chance to meet a lovely woman," I said smiling, with little hope she'd buy that one. These ladies strode through life like Harvard MBA's looking for their next promotion. "Scout's honor." I held up three fingers.

Kristyn seemed to be winnowing this chaff to see if there was any wheat, then said, "In a hundred words or less, what would you write about me?"

Sometimes even I get tossed a big fat, home run pitch.

We grinned at one another, challenge issued and accepted.

Taking in a breath, I said, "Mid-heading-to-upper management in a Fortune 500 company. Nothing stuffy; probably advertising."

Her eyes wrinkled at the corners, and the effect was like a red cape waved at a bull.

"You have a big, floppy-eared dog rescued from the pound. You like Sunday afternoons at bookstores, sipping cappuccino and giggling at random passages in trashy romance novels—leisure time well spent in your opinion."

From the floors below, a ruckus exploded.

"Midnight!" we echoed and scrambled to our feet to gaze out the tower windows. The lights remained on, still twinkling.

Kristyn turned and with a hug, we shared a celebratory kiss. Though modest and tentative, it felt promising.

Horns honked, bottle rockets arched across the sky and from below rose the clanging hubbub of people greeting the New Year.

"We need to make a wish for the New Year," she insisted brightly.

I knew mine.

Tossing caution to the wind, I pulled her back and we tangled like vines in a trellised arbor. In the midst of this ferment, my brain skit-tered before finally ticking off my wish list for the new millennium. I took a step back but held her shoulders with outstretched hands, silently formulating what I hoped, no believed, the new millennium had in store for us.

Kristyn and I surrender to the perils of love.
We honeymoon at a Montana dude ranch.
A big, slobbery rescue mutt makes three.
Even if computers blow their circuits, life continues on merrily.
Eventually I write a story or two worth reading.
And—surprise—a baby girl makes four and for lots of fun.
We're happy evermore as two-peas-in-a-pod.

Something wanted to come over me, and I let it. For once. Step-ping close, I wrap Kristyn in my arms, my hands racing over the in-viting nooks and crannies when she suddenly stiffens. From pleasure, or . . . ?

"What on earth?" I manage to sputter. Something definitely not part of standard issue female anatomy brings my fevered grope to a halt.

"It's my gun," she says flatly. "In case you get rowdy."

Transparently, my face indicates some rapid internal re-calculations and she's clearly pleased with the effect.

"I'm a detective. Gotta wear it, even off-duty."

"Oh," I say, unnerved.

She smiles. "So, what's your next move, cowboy?"

The end

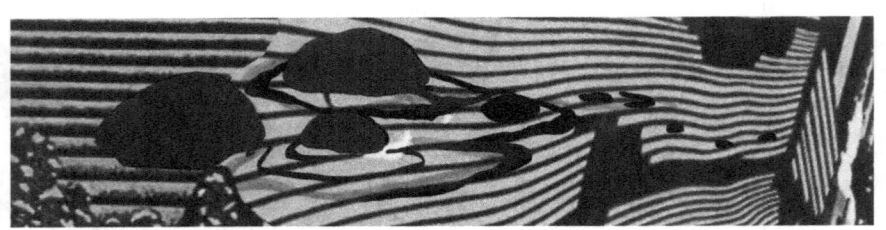

The Days That Are No More

"Last days of freedom?"

I have to practically yell to cover the distance between us. PJ keeps at least five steps ahead, texting whenever she thinks I'm not watching.

I thought we could wander around downtown and share some father-daughter time. Ever since the divorce I've been a lousy part-time dad, but I want to change that.

Truth be told, though, I wasn't much of a full-time dad and it's all I can do to keep the guilt at bay. Like the time I forgot to pick her up after soccer and, lugging all her schoolbooks and gear she had to hike two miles to get home in the dark. Or, when I was late to a father-daughter school dance and hadn't had time to change into the requisite formal wear. Even I wince at the excuses I make to her and myself and sometimes how callous I can be.

But some of it is her fault, too. She has no trouble communicating in cyberspace, but can't manage a few civil words with her father. Fifteen years old, lanky and loose-limbed, she strolls a little further before stopping, pretending her father doesn't exist.

"Hey, school starts next week, doesn't it?" I try again, confident in that I happen to know this to be a fact.

She finally turns, looking bored and contemptuous.

"I'm surprised you know." Her sharp tone clashes with her slack posture.

When I was young and didn't give a damn, I stood like that to piss off my father. I guess girls have attained equality with boys at least in that sphere, how dismissive they are to their fathers. No more trying to please Dad like when she was younger.

"I try to keep up," I answer mildly. I wish I could be sure what would pull us together.

"Yeah, right," she sneers, slouching a little more.

I'd asked her to lay off texting this morning to give us a chance to "catch up." She glances not-so-subtly at her, for-the-moment inactive cell phone hand.

"Look . . ." I start to say, but close my mouth tightly. I already feel weary. PJ has a right to be angry with me, god knows. We live in the same town, and you'd think I could make it to a few of her after-school activities once in a while. When I remember to check my inbox, I answer her emails but texting and all the app crap is lost on me. Impatient, she walks away smartly flicking her brown hair over her shoulders and adjusting the sleeves of her blouse. In only a moment she's way ahead of me.

At Wideman's, she lingers in front of the store window sneaking looks at her cell phone. Two stores from her, I stop. The window display in front of me has an assortment of old stuff. I'm only vaguely interested until I spot a grouping of shop-worn drafting equipment like I used in high school.

Scared, I take my seat in the back row. Over the stage a large orange and blue banner proclaims, Baltimore Polytechnic Institute. There must be two hundred boys in this auditorium. Each wears a pressed shirt and a new tie. The older boys sport chunky class rings and you know the smart ones by the slide ruler hanging from their hips like a gunslinger. A man dressed like my father speaks into the microphone. "H.L. Mencken, the 'Sage of Baltimore,'" he booms proudly, "came here as a boy and left a man. Our proud tradition is to prepare you for the future."

PJ walks on but not as quickly as before. Has she changed her mind about this day together? Maybe giving her old man some slack for a change? The morning sun is just now warm enough to infuse me with meager hope. Somewhere nearby coffee is brewing as I ease closer to her.

"I've decided to become an actress." She turns with this sudden announcement.

I'm taken aback. "That's great!" I enthuse loudly, grateful for any connection, "You'll be famous!"

"Why can't we ever have a normal conversation?" she says, embarrassed.

Clueless as usual, I have no idea how to respond except with anger. It seems as if she deliberately tries to piss me off despite my meager efforts to be a decent father.

"Because, young lady," I hiss, "you won't let me."

"Fuck you," she says flatly and stares at me, her steely eyes daring me to issue a stern reprimand.

I flinch instead, and every sensible thought scatters from my head like confetti. Again, I am not here on the sidewalk with her, but flashing back to my father's clumsy attempts at parenting.

I wait, as usual, for the old man to lower his morning newspaper and lecture me about school. Doesn't he know that baggy pants, a white shirt, tie, and Vitalis hair are pure Stone Age? After another sip of coffee he starts in, "How do you expect to ever make anything of yourself? Do you want to throw away your future?"

The laughter of young children flutters from a second-story window and snags my attention. It's hard to recall the image of PJ when she was little, full of giggles and wiggles, and I thought we had all the time in the world for me to figure her out. To figure me out. To figure us out.

Before I can respond, PJ scuttles across the intersection against the traffic light. I jog walk to catch up and make amends. But my bum knee gives out just as she turns back toward me from the far curb. Her eyes bug out as I pitch forward and jam my hands and knees into the still cool asphalt.

PJ dashes back to help me and deftly plucks a tiny stone embedded in my palm. "Your pants are torn," she says.

I want to brush them but say weakly, "Hope you never get this old and creaky."

She responds by tapping on her cell phone as if consulting an electronic psychic about age and health. Then, apparently getting an answer, and—to my surprise—she firmly takes my elbow and leads us slowly back to the sidewalk and down a different block.

"My latest app," PJ says, holding up her phone. "Java Now," she announces as if doing an infomercial.

"That's one smart app," I say, though I have only a vague notion what it does other than it will guide us to a place of refuge.

In three minutes we sit facing each other, her trusty phone now resting on the small round table waiting to perform another magic trick. I wonder if it has a translation app for father-daughter conversations. Now that would be a money maker.

"Can we start over?" I meekly offer, as the server returns with my amaretto coffee and her hot chocolate topped with whipped cream.

She shrugs and absent-mindedly spins the phone on the tabletop.

"Everything is different nowadays," I say. "We didn't have cell phones, computers or cable TV. At your age, I had no idea what I wanted to do."

I'm fighting to keep my mind in this moment, with her.

The school guidance counselor riffles through a big pile of manila folders until he finds mine. "I think you're wasting your time here at Polytechnic. I have a buddy, a foreman, down at Bethlehem Steel. I could get you into their apprenticeship program. Your future would be secure and, best of all, no more homework." He laughs and I laugh but don't say anything.

"Before computers and cell phones?" She says quizzically though with obvious humor.

"That was just after the electric light was invented," I answer.

"Right after the really dark ages," she manages to say, giggling.

This is the first lightness between us in a long time and she lifts her cup. "Cheers!"

Blowing on her hot chocolate she seems to turn inward. Then, her tongue flicks at the whipped cream and I flinch involuntarily, supplying the erotic imagery that wouldn't even occur to her. Or, would it? Sex is all over TV and the Internet for any kid who cares to watch.

Pushing that aside I say, "I *still* don't know what I want," and laugh.

She stops mid-lick, eyes fixed on me. I wonder what I've done now. In this moment I glimpse across the years because of a tiny curl of her lip. She's about to be silly for Dad. On cue, PJ pokes her nose into the whipped cream and comes up grinning.

I smile, feeling a hint of optimism about our future.

"We need to do something fun," I say.

"Like what?"

"Remember Princess PJ?" I ask, recalling when she was eight and we went shopping at secondhand stores for clothes and cheap jewelry to make a Halloween costume.

"The contest," her voice is quick and girlish.

"Right." I don't quite know where to take this. Unexpectedly, she intervenes.

"We could shop for hippie clothes. They're so in." Hoping it's true, I say, "There must be a secondhand shop in the neighborhood?"

She picks up her phone and begins tapping. "There's a bunch," she says.

We work our way through several stores finding only odd bits of not too great clothing. The elation is quickly draining from both of us. I'm limping and her mood is going flat, the last bit of her fizz almost gone. It won't be long before I can kiss this day goodbye and add another tic mark to the column, "Failure as a Father."

At the end of another block of low rent shops, PJ stops and consults her phone. "Let me see," she mumbles, then points. "That way," she says emphatically.

After a few zigzags through narrow streets, we're standing in front of another funky store.

"This is where Amy got the coolest denim jacket," she says.

"Peace," PJ says to the store clerk as we enter, raising her fingers in a "V." He's tall and thin with long hair and a toothy, welcoming smile. I follow stupidly, also raising my fingers in a "V."

Tables and rickety shelves are heaped with tchotchkes from the sixties and seventies along with crowded racks of clothes that defined my generation. I marvel at lava lamps, a VW steering wheel, an eight-track tape player and Beatles posters in black and white. In a nearby nook, PJ paws at clothes as I make my way toward her. A three-inch wide polka dot tie catches my attention. Holding it up I say, "I swear I wore this in high school."

"Still a nerd." She shakes her head and returns to her retro foray.

Wandering down another isle, I keep an eye on PJ as she checks out different outfits. Under some junk on a table I spot a slide rule in its leather case. "Perfect!" I shout and quickly loop it through my belt. It was THE trademark of all the engineering students at Polytechnic, though I never got the hang of it.

Over the top of a rack of dresses I spy on her. She's busy knotting a flowing reddish scarf around her waist. Behind her is a tall, three-panel mirror where she checks her progress, fussing and pulling, making faces, totally absorbed in herself.

I'm mesmerized. She's dressed in an off-white gown, delicately trimmed with cream-colored lace. A fringed paisley shawl drapes artfully over her shoulders. PJ gathers up the long skirt, scooping the train over her forearm and spins around. Our eyes meet.

I laugh in amazement. Long live the rock-and-roll generation and how, here and now, it brings us together.

All in a moment, I've finally seen the future—PJ's and mine.

And I'm ready.

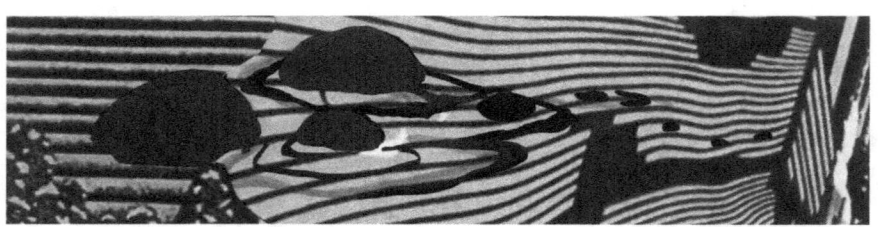

Alone in the Galaxy

Twinkly stars danced in the night sky above the Ford Galaxie 500. It must have been some great car when it was new. I imagined its black paint and chrome all bright and shiny, and its big V-8 powerful enough to fly right up into the stars.

Instead, I used the old junk car as my hideout to get away from the trailer while they drank and fought late into the night. After dinner tonight, I came out here with a dish of food for Duke. He's old and crippled and not much use as a dog. But he always keeps me company and I can talk to him without any problem. That's why I don't want to lose him; he's my only friend. Without him I'm on my own.

I thought about that silent V-8 engine under the hood and wished I knew how to get it roaring again. Maybe I could learn how to fix it by watching the mechanics down at Jimmy's Garage. Then, with Duke hanging out the passenger side window sniffing the breeze, we'd blast out of these mountains and never look in the rearview mirror ever again.

Duke really belongs to Buddy, Maw's boyfriend, but he didn't pay him no attention anymore. I'd been taking care of him ever since me,

Maw and my little brother Junior moved in with Buddy. Before him, we were living at the Harpers Ferry KOA campground where we was left high and dry by Junior's Pop. One morning, he went out for cigarettes and was gone for good without so much as a-go-to-holy-hell.

Maw latched onto Buddy pretty quick. He was a lot older than her and lived nearby in a trailer on two acres. Doing odd jobs at the KOA and cutting firewood was how he made spending money.

I never fit in that cobbled together family. Junior was like a son while I was treated like dirt and Maw had her ups and downs depending on I didn't know what. Lately they'd been on the outs and were drinkin' more. That's when Buddy would try and start fights just to prove something. Luckily, I was big enough to hold him off. Barely.

One night I was getting Duke's dinner ready, glopping the stinky mess from a tin can into an old Hudson hubcap I use for his bowl. The tiny kitchen of Buddy's trailer was open to the little dining room where Junior and him sat as usual, elbow to elbow, him drinking and Junior watching. A small piece of counter separated the two rooms. I always ate standing at the counter, stuck in the middle. Maw stood on the kitchen side behind me jammed up against a stool. She stayed as far away as she could from Buddy except late at night when they shared a bed. Then he made enough noise to make sure we knew Maw belonged to him no matter how hard she fought.

"I oughta get rid of that flea-bag dog. Too damn many free-loaders," Buddy talked to his can of Old German. Junior followed Buddy's every move with his big round eyes. About the only time they were apart was when they slept. I shared a room with Junior but he peed in the bed, so I slept on the floor in an old military surplus sleeping bag that leaked tiny feathers.

I pictured Buddy dragging Duke off into the woods and firing a bullet through his skull, and put my fork down.

"Too goddamn many mouths." Buddy spit out his words so they were aimed at Maw. She pretended like she didn't hear and kept on stirring some stew, probably rabbit or squirrel again. Buddy loved to hunt both. Junior went along and retrieved the bloody dead critters almost as good as any dog. It didn't matter how Maw cooked them, they tasted worse than rotten grease.

"Hear me?" Buddy hollered at me and, at the same time, smacked Junior on the back of his head. "Boy, can't you see I need another beer?" He let out a big "haw, haw" at Junior's confusion. Junior wiggled past me and Maw to get to the fridge without touching either of us. Even though he was fourteen, only a year younger than me, he still looked like a little kid. Acted like one, too. "Slow," was what they called him, but he seemed all right to me. The handle on the fridge was broke and you had to work it with a screwdriver to get it opened. Junior had lots of practice and did it no sweat.

"Maybe tonight I'll do me some huntin' close to home. A million slant-eyes eat dog, so it must be tasty." Buddy spoke like it was to no one in particular but I knew it was me he was talking to. He knew Duke and I were buddies and he'd been making noises about getting a coon dog pup to replace Duke.

I snuck a look for his .22 rifle that was leaning in the corner where he usually kept it.

His squinty pig eyes were on me. "You got somethin' to say, boy?" he demanded in his mean voice, like he was lookin' for a fight or something. "Think you're hot shit 'cause you're gettin' a little hair on your chin?" He stared hard at me but I avoided his look.

Junior slid back in next to Buddy and handed him the beer. "I think little Junior here could kick your ass." He patted Junior's head.

Buddy was pushing me around like the tough guys at school. I knew not to do anything, not 'til I filled out some more. My day was coming soon when Buddy would have his hands full. Until then, I'd have to eat his crap.

"Yessirree, one less useless critter around this dump wouldn't hardly be missed." Buddy grabbed Junior by the hair, pushed his head down against the table and held it there. I pretended nothing was going on. Junior didn't move a muscle and breathed loud and hard with his nose mashed against the table. "This here dummy can't even remember to open my beer. Guess he needs more training." He grabbed Junior by the hair on the back of his head and pulled his face off the table, which made Junior squirm.

Maw looked up from the stew. "Leave the boy be," she said, but didn't sound like she cared one way or another. Stirring the pot of stew seemed to be all she could handle.

"Aww, I'm sorry, real sorry. Did I hurt youuu?" Buddy made a big deal, mussing Junior's hair like they was best friends. A slimy wet spot glistened on the table from Junior's mouth. "Old Buddy didn't mean to hurt the dummy," he said sing-song-y. Then he put his arm around Junior and hugged him. Junior looked at him with those wide dog eyes and grinned big as day.

"How about you getting me the opener?" He was talking to me

just as nice as you please. That worried me but I was getting fed up. Maw didn't look my way and sipped a beer like there was nobody else in the trailer with her.

When he talked directly at me, I felt stuck.

"I'm talking to you, boooy. Not that good-for-nothing bitch." He unsheathed his big knife from his belt and quickly poked two holes in the top of the beer can. "I've had dogs smarter than her." He took a big gulp making foam spew out and slide down the can onto the table top.

"I got to feed the dog," I said, sucking in air fast like I was running.

"That reminds me of why we're having this little talk." He drained his beer. "Another," he shouted, holding up his empty beer can.

Junior got him one and remembered to open it using his own thin bladed knife. The one he used to skin squirrels and rabbits.

"Good boy." He patted Junior on the head. "Now, where was I?"

"You can't get rid of Duke." I tried to keep my voice low and steady like I wasn't afraid. Whenever he heard my voice shake, it made him come after me with his fists.

The pig eyes got narrow. "Just cause your dick gets hard don't make you the boss." Buddy was fingering the big knife on the table. "Maybe we ought to settle this once and for all."

Junior eased slowly away from him like a slinking dog expecting to get kicked.

"I ain't the boss," I croaked, scared shitless he'd pick up the knife. Give him enough beer and he could get right nasty and explode.

He smiled and for just a second I let down my guard. Quick as a flash he threw his beer catching me in the shoulder. It hurt some but I was almost happy because he didn't throw the knife. The can rattled around on the kitchen floor, foam squirting everywhere. My knees were shaking so bad I hung tightly to the counter to keep from falling.

"Guess you ain't man enough to do anything," he spat, his voice loud and his face showing one big shit-eating grin. He turned to Junior who was frozen in a crouch, arms covering his head. "How's about another beer? I seem to have lost mine somewheres," he said like we were all just yakking.

Buddy picked up the big knife and started paring his nails, dropping the dirty yellow shavings on the table. Uncoiling, Junior stood and eased over to the fridge and didn't take his eyes off Buddy.

Sometimes there was this calm before the worst happened like he was trying to decide something.

I felt like I could puke.

As if a storm had passed, though, everything settled down quick after Buddy'd made his point. That was the thing. You never knew which way it would go.

I gathered up the dog's food without turning my back on him and was glad to be gone. Outside it was getting dark and some stars were popping out when I slipped away.

I walked through the weeds and junk on the dirt path that went out back to the Galaxie. It seemed like Buddy collected only broken-down machinery and old cars that didn't run. Just about the whole two acres was covered with junk. That was okay, though, because it gave me plenty of places to hide. Besides, I could find the Galaxie with my eyes closed and nobody else could bother me.

I slid in behind the bent steering wheel and set the food down next to me. Duke struggled up on his forelegs to eat as best he could. A zillion stars come out before he finished. Then, I had to help him get out of the car so he could do his business before we settled in for the evening.

Now we were alone in the Galaxie.

Duke was like a real human to me though he mostly grunted and sighed and stank up the place. It didn't matter because he was all the company I needed. Why'd Buddy turn against this old dog? I wanted to ask Duke how that'd happened. Buddy had raised him up from a puppy and he'd been a good dog until he got old. No point in askin'. Duke was snoring now that his stomach was full.

I slid my fingers along the hard nubs of the slick steering wheel, thinking some more. Seemed like nothing counted for nothing in this world. Paw left me and Maw when I was two. And then Junior's paw up and leaves us after twelve years, like we meant nothing to him. Buddy's acting no better except he'll keep Junior and maybe Maw.

I scratched Duke's ear a little. "He don't want either of us." The dog groaned, like he knew that too.

Gripping the steering wheel tight as I could I yelled, "Move, you goddamn son-of-a-bitch!"

Duke lifted his head and I worried that he thought I'd yelled at him. I tried to calm him by saying, "I promise I'll never let him lay a hand on you."

It was all I could do to keep from crying over this old, broken-down dog and a good-for-nothing car. I wanted us to be speeding down a highway with the bad times behind and miles and miles of empty blacktop ahead.

Things settled down for a while. Buddy got busy with getting the campgrounds ready for winter, and left me alone. But when the weather turned real cold and work at the campground got slow I started worrying again. Idle time was bad on Buddy.

There'd been a cold rain all day and nothing to do. We stayed cooped up in the trailer. Right after lunch Maw and Buddy started drinking beer. By four I was getting a bad feeling and decided to grab some food and go out early to stay with Duke. They weren't too loud yet, but the noise was rising and my gut told me to git. I eased out of the front room and left them arguing over some TV program.

I slapped two jelly sandwiches together and was spooning food into Duke's dish when Junior came up to me. One look at him and I knew trouble was here. He tried to talk but like usual words got jumbled in that crooked mouth of his. Then he started pulling me towards the back door and I had to push him away.

"Goddamn you," I said real angry. Now I'd have to take care of Junior and things were moving too fast. We had to run and I'd sort out what to do with Junior later.

"Let's git," I tossed the jelly sandwiches on top of the dog food, grabbed the dish in one hand and pushed Junior with the other. "Faster, dammit!" I wanted us out the door and in the old car before things really blew up. The yelling would go on and we'd be hunkered down with Duke and the jelly sandwiches away from all that, watching the cloudy sky darken until night settled around us.

But it was too late. They whirled into the room, hissing and screeching like two cats going at it. We were trapped and I was so pissed at Junior that I forgot to be scared and swore I'd get even with him. But for now all I could do was try and make myself invisible.

Maw and Buddy squared off like the start of a schoolyard fight.

"You see that bitch again and I'm leavin'," Maw screamed, hands balled into fists, face red as a tomato, her jaw sticking out.

"Leave? I'm throwing you out!" He started for the bedroom. Maw blocked his way and they shoved and pushed, forcing all of us back into the kitchen. Junior and me scrambled out of the way trying to stay ahead of them. This just made me really mad and I'd about had it with all of them.

They broke apart and squared off again, not an inch separating them. I saw for the first time that he wasn't a big man. Maw outweighed him and was almost a head taller. I guess I'd never noticed them that close together to even think about it.

"I'll see any bitch I want to see." He thumped her on the chest with a pointed finger.

"That's it, I'm leaving. I'm taking Junior. You can keep him." Maw looked at me and then stooped over to get Junior.

I felt an explosion in my chest, like fire.

"Like hell," Buddy jumped, pushing her off balance pinning her against the stove. He reached for Junior. I shoved Junior to them tired of the whole mess. Buddy pushed her down and snatched Junior, yanking him up one handed.

"He's mine!" she screamed and sprang up to claim him, but froze. Buddy had his free hand on the big knife strapped to his belt. He smiled.

"Now you're mine, bitch." He drew his hand up into a tight fist, the diamond horseshoe ring twinkling. Out of nowhere, Maw came up with a pair of scissors. Buddy hesitated, time enough for my move.

I grabbed a ketchup bottle from the counter and used it like a club on the back of her head. This made Buddy's jaw drop and his hands come up like he knew he was next. The scissors had spun across the floor out of sight as I dropped the bottle. It broke on the counter and made a sorry mess—ketchup all over the place and a bunch of coffee cups smashed. Pieces of busted china skittered everywhere, on the counter and onto the floor. I didn't care one bit.

Then it got dead quiet.

The old man didn't move a muscle, like he was a statue. Before he could even think about swinging, I took two quick steps and kicked him square in the nuts. He doubled over moaning and dropped with a thunk onto the linoleum next to Maw.

"Goddamn sonofabitch," I hollered at the top of my lungs while kicking him in the ribs until my legs got too tired to do it anymore. Blood dribbled out his mouth. His breath was short and raggedy. Maw's was the same. From the looks of it, you'd think I'd killed them both. I could have. Maybe I should have.

I turned to Junior and he stared wide-eyed like I was crazy. With the heels of both hands I slammed him up hard against the cupboards and he sank to the floor in a whimpering squeak. Grabbing the .22 and the box of shells and picking up the hubcap with Duke's dinner, I slipped out the door. Stars sparkled above a thin haze of clouds in the cool evening air.

I gave Duke his last dinner and went back to the shed to get a shovel. Digging kept me busy for a while, but the deeper I dug the more my thoughts went back and forth. I jabbed at the hard-packed dirt again and again until I settled on the truth: Duke was old and crippled and he wasn't Buddy's anymore. I couldn't trust that Buddy wouldn't be cruel to him when I wasn't around. He'd torment the poor animal for spite, figuring that was the only thing left that could hurt me.

Duke finished dinner and I took him out to do his business. I sat on the edge of the grave with Duke across my lap, hoping I was doing the right thing. If I sat there too long, I knew my thoughts would turn again. Quickly, I got him comfortable in the hole.

I pulled the trigger, and the bullet exploded from the chamber.

Once I'd smoothed the dirt on top of the grave I felt a lot better, like there was nothing left to keep me here.

That done, I got in behind the wheel of the car and looked straight ahead afraid to look at the empty passenger's seat. Duke's smell hung in the air and I breathed deeply until my lungs were filled with him. This made no difference and I wondered if I shouldn't join him and be shut of everything. The clouds were gone and I tried to lose myself in the bigness of the night sky while wishing that Duke was a pup again and I was with him from the start.

I musta' conked out for a long time, because the stars had changed to sunlight. I looked at the empty place beside me and knew there was no going back. I'd made it this far with Duke for company.

Now, it was just me, and I wasn't afraid to be on my own.

I gripped the steering wheel and imagined the car brand new, the radio playing, all the gauges flickering, and the big V-8 pounding under the hood. I'm sixteen, maybe seventeen, barreling down the highway the speedometer dead on seventy with the music cranked-up higher than the wind and, for a little while, I don't feel alone.

The end.

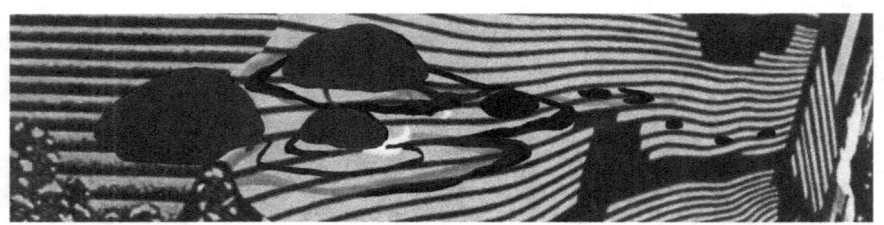

Feeling Lucky

An old, rusted-out bomb of a car cut a squiggly track through the snow-covered road, angled into the lot and stopped outside the plate glass window of Carson's Country Store.

It had been a hunker-down kind of day where people wouldn't venture out unless they were desperate for a pack of smokes or a six-pack. There'd been no customers since noon and, with dusk falling, this car could either be an interesting diversion or really bad news.

Carson watched from his stool behind the front counter, thinking about bald tires and blown-out mufflers. Over the years, plenty of lonely hard-luck cases had coasted onto his parking lot with the engine sputtering and not enough spare change for a pack of discount cigarettes.

He always thought of it as a crap-shoot, what anyone stopping here would want, especially since the new by-pass took away the traffic. Sometimes just directions and not a nickel spent. Sometimes there were lots of other motives, and more than once after dealing with a hard-luck case Carson had said to Mabel, "I should have been a social worker."

A lone, husky woman got out of the cancerous Chevy and high-stepped through the falling snow toward the door, two long braids swinging wildly. Faded blue jeans were tucked into work boots and a bulky, cable-knit sweater showed under a puffy vest. One pocket of the unbuttoned vest sagged, and Carson guessed it was loaded with crap women usually carried, unless it was a Saturday night special.

Easing off the tall stool, he slowly unkinked his old bones and focused as if he was in his tree stand evaluating his quarry. *Old hippie*, he decided and sat back down blowing out a long breath, "Peace and love."

A smile briefly lit his face at the prospect of a diversion and, just maybe, some fun. His pistol remained on the shelf in its holster and his empty right hand moved to rest on the counter. Women, he reminded himself, could be just as devious as men. Tugging open the heavy door, the woman whooshed in on a wave of frigid air.

She could have been a feedstore pin-up, Carson mused, he could see her posed leaning against a vintage Ford tractor, rosy cheeked and enough padding in all the right places to keep a farmer happy on most any night. Smiling for just a second, he added the caption, "A Girl Who Knows How to Handle Old Equipment!"

"I just knew you were open," she said smiling brightly, and bopped right up to the counter. "The *I Ching* told me."

Carson deliberately kept a neutral face, deciding she wasn't bad looking for a New Age Momma—though around her kooky edges he sensed darkness. Definitely after something, he thought. Cash, smokes, booze, love or e) all of the above?

"The *I Ching*," she said again, when he didn't respond, "*The Book of Changes.*"

Her bright, chatty voice thawed Carson a little. Although he missed the old days when customers and gossip were plentiful and Mabel puttered around the store, he reminded himself, *Keep up your guard.*

"I'm due for a change," he answered, looking around the vacant store with its meagerly stocked shelves, splintery floors, and musty smell of decline. Outside, the snow had begun to fall faster again. Likely, anyone going someplace was already there and wouldn't venture out.

"Cosmic," she responded, eyes sparkling above flushed cheeks, as if they'd made a meaningful connection.

"Comic," he deadpanned, wanting to stretch out this encounter, though he couldn't see how this would come to anything good and might end badly.

His little joke seemed to lighten her some more and he wondered if she thought him ripe for plucking. Mabel had been the soft one when it came to hard-luck women, always sending them along with a few bucks, a pat on the shoulder, and a goodbye, saying, "You take care, honey; things'll get better."

He felt the stab he always felt when Mabel's face and voice rose to mind.

"Truth is, I've had some bad Karma lately," she said, her voice going flat. An embarrassed 'poor me' smile appeared. Then, she perked up again a little. "But, things'll turn around soon."

Carson's face remained impassive, belying his surprise at hearing Mabel's faint echo more than a year after she'd passed. Had this woman been here before? Deep down the feeling grew that this could be a con game. After waiting a few beats, he asked, "Who's Karma anyway?"

She looked at the ceiling for a moment, apparently thinking. *Part of her act*, Carson figured. Mabel believed in helping the needy and it gave her something to pray over. He did neither.

"Not 'who.' It's a 'what.' It's like something happens because of something you've done in this life or a past life," she said, her face becoming more animated as if she knew Carson would understand the concept. "Like a repayment," she added helpfully.

Carson blinked at her hopeful face, puzzled by her crazy notions. To him, dead was dead. Mabel had proved that, though sometimes he did feel like she'd just left a room and might return at any moment. *Too much dead time*, he decided.

His stare must have unnerved her, because her gaze dropped to the countertop. Carson wondered if she could read his Karma from the dings in its worn oak surface.

Not wanting her to leave, he asked, "How bad?"

Her yellow feather earrings swung gently he noticed for the first time, and clusters of silver bangles ringed her wrists. Mabel had never worn jewelry except her gold wedding band. She was skinny-as-a-rail, practical, and could cook one hell of a great beef brisket.

"First," she began with a sharp intake of breath, "my old man split when I started getting into spirituality."

Carson didn't care to listen, really. By being polite all he was gambling on was some reasonable conversation to fill the empty winter afternoon a little, not New Age bull crap or a hard luck story. Mostly he missed the sounds Mabel made clomping up and down the cellar stairs, clanking pots and pans in the kitchen, humming to herself out in the garden. After her passing, he'd closed the home place and moved to the apartment upstairs with alien night sounds like vibrating car music while someone slammed the balky soda machine or took a leak against the building.

"Hey?" she waved a hand.

Carson refocused and noted her concern for his mental lapse. She smiled at his return to the present. "Some tough luck, huh?" he managed to say.

"Yeah," she continued, "then the farm I was renting got sold. My car died, and then naturally I got fired for missing work."

At this point Mabel would have offered some kind of help, Carson thought. But his motives weren't pure and, truth be told, he was kind of attracted to this kooky woman; she couldn't have been more opposite to Mabel. Besides, maybe she was a little interested in him, or so it seemed to him. Why else was she hanging around?

"What kind of work did you do?" An extra hand around the store would help and some female company could be a plus.

"I worked in a New Age bookstore," she said. "The owner was only out for the money and didn't appreciate my spiritual journey either."

No, not Walmart material, he decided. At least she'd had a job.

Purposefully stepping closer to the counter, she suddenly reached around to her back.

Spooked, Carson hopped backwards off his high stool, the pistol left behind on the shelf under the counter. With broad shoulders, at his full six feet, two inches height he still looked impressive even with his beach-ball gut. Had he gambled wrong on her?

In turn, she quick-stepped back, as if afraid he would try to grab her.

"Why'd you do that?" she huffed, when he made no more moves. "You scared the crap out of me." She unfolded the paper she'd pulled from her rear pocket.

Her eyes had hardened and shoulders squared, which told him that she'd fight if need be.

"Sorry," he said, "my leg started cramping." Carson rubbed his thigh, pretending it was the truth. *Must think I'm a jumpy old fart*, he concluded, after deciding she could take care of herself.

"Not going to shoot me, are you?" she smiled, softening somewhat, obviously eager to show him the paper.

Grinning back, he let himself ease down onto the stool. Good thing for his bum hand he decided, or the gun would have come out. Besides, she might have one herself, and it would have been another O.K. Corral.

"I'm training to be a Reflexologist," she said, smoothing the paper out on the counter.

"Really?" he replied, confused by this change in direction. It must be some new kind of exercise program.

"Yes." She picked up the paper. "See?"

"The Answer to Life's Problems." Carson skimmed over the printed announcement, 'Dr. Deana was giving free demonstrations, etc.' Just New Age mumbo-jumbo. "Are you the doctor?"

"No! I'm Harvest Moon, a student of Dr. D's," she said proudly. "Is there someplace in your window I can put this poster?"

Once Ms. Moon accomplished what she's come for, Carson laid odds, she'd take off and he'd head upstairs alone. The best he could offer was, "Need some tape?"

She took the dispenser and scouted a location. Her name, Harvest Moon, made him think of a big fuzzy orange autumn moon, the smell of wood smoke, and the home he dearly missed.

"Hel-loo-*oo*," she said, when she was back in front of the counter.

"Hi," Carson reacted, now rattled by his mental meandering. He didn't even care if she turned out to be bad news. What good did it do to keep the dice in your pocket and never roll 'em?

"Guess I'll be on my way," she said, without moving.

He swallowed hard. The cash drawer was hers if she'd stay a while.

"The snowplow should be along soon," Carson offered. "Say, could that re-flex-whatever help?" He held up his bum wrist, making a bid. "Hurt it in October and it kept me from deer hunting."

"I have posters to hang," Harvest Moon said, looking out to the snow-covered car. "Maybe I could stop back?"

"How about a cup of coffee?" he offered.

"Tea?" she asked, the arch of her eyebrow said no way.

"Lipton's?" he said, because it was the only kind he knew.

Harvest Moon made a *yuck* face. "Any herbal tea?"

Somewhere in Carson's apartment was a sample pack of fruity teas that had come in the mail.

"Tell you what," he started, "I'll make you a cup if . . . " That was as far as his mind would go. He felt old and too stuffed with Mabel memories.

"If *what?*"

"Nothing." Carson felt his face getting hot. He slumped a little on the stool.

"You don't look so good," she said taking his hand firmly as a nurse would, to steady him. "Your whole arm is tense."

She began to work the muscles, tendons and flesh of his lower arm, wrist and hand with capable sinewy fingers, watching his face the whole time.

It was better than anything he could remember. The heat from her ministrations did wonders; it was a good hurt. He managed to say, "That Reflexology sure works."

"Didn't you read the poster?" she scolded mildly. "Reflexology is for the feet."

"Well, it feels good anyway."

"This bad wrist must make it hard for you to run this place," she said, slowly kneading into the muscle. She didn't mention his age or the coating of dust everywhere. "You got any help?"

"Naw," Carson mumbled, silently praying she'd never stop.

"Guess business is tough with all these gas-n-go's popping up like weeds?"

He nodded agreement and kept quiet. She placed his hand gently back on the counter.

"Ever thought of selling health foods? Vitamins?"

Carson mulled over this left field notion. "I wouldn't know the first thing about it."

"Well," she chirped, "I worked in a health food store after I dropped out of college. Always wanted to start my own store."

Carson wasn't ready to peddle tofu or organic eggs and grass-fed beef. "Maybe you could stay around and give me some pointers?" He guessed this was the answer she was angling for and made his bid.

"Are you deaf?" she shot back. "I told you I'm studying Reflexology."

This wasn't going anywhere, and Carson knew he'd never get along with a kooky, vegetarian foot person.

"The snow's letting up," he said finally.

"Yeah," she frowned and headed to the front door, but turned back. "I don't know Reflexology yet. I'm, like, real enthusiastic when I first get into something, but I don't know . . . . "

Ah, he thought, *maybe there's still a chance.*

"Hey, Mr. Carson, what are you thinking?" Perhaps she'd seen his disappointment or just sensed an opportunity. Perhaps she'd just keep hopping from one thing to another and never settle into a career.

Does it matter? "My friends call me Carson."

She nodded. "You know, I might try massage therapy. Reflexology is so limited."

"You'd be damned good," he said, holding up his bad hand.

Loud, gritty scraping and flashing yellow lights from the highway snowplow distracted them for a moment. The road would be passable all the way to Charles Town and the one-armed bandits, roulette wheels and card games that never ever closed, a gambler's heaven.

"Just another pipe dream. Guess I'm just trying my luck to see what works," she sighed.

As she turned once again toward the door, Carson decided she'd rather be taking her chances down the road; probably feed her last quarter into the slots. Sensing a momentary hesitation, he asked, "Feeling lucky?"

As she casually looked around Carson's apartment, he was glad that, by habit, he kept things neat and clean. Between them on the rough pine kitchen table, Carson placed a sample pack of twelve herbal teas and an old black metal cash box. A city phonebook could fit inside and it appeared to be as heavy.

"What's in the box?" Harvest Moon asked intrigued.

Carson knew the old cash box looked like it should be stuffed full with old greenbacks gone wrinkly soft, just the thing an old miserly widower would have. When he'd returned with the box, Harvest Moon had assumed a new position on the plank-bottom chair. One hand was tucked in her coat pocket, again making him wonder if she was clutching a small revolver or a switchblade.

"Could be something. I'm not sure," he said tapping the lid with his index finger.

"What's the game?" she finally asked.

If she'd have a cup of tea in his apartment, Carson had promised a game of chance.

"Remember," she added, "no funny business. You swore on a stack of bibles."

"We cut cards and high card wins," Carson said as he fumbled a deck from his shirt pocket then offered it to Harvest Moon.

Slowly, she let go of whatever was in her pocket and took the cards in both hands, shuffling like a seasoned player. "I don't have any stake for this game."

Carson laughed. "I have the steak. You lose, you cook it."

Mid-shuffle Harvest Moon stopped; it had taken a moment to figure out his proposition. "How do you know I can cook?"

"You take your chances, I'll take mine."

She studied his face and saw he was serious. "What's in the box?" she asked again.

Opening the lid revealed a miniature pawnshop that might have been shaken by an earthquake.

"Are they real?" she asked, sounding dubious. Harvest Moon peered wide-eyed as if looking into an unlocked bank vault.

"Mabel, my late wife," he began, "was a soft touch for some of the road weary who've dragged in over the years. For spot cash, a few cartons of smokes or whatever, you wouldn't believe some of the things they'd offer—a diamond ring, a fancy watch, rare coins or a piece of jewelry."

Harvest Moon stared at the booty, calculating. After a time, when the math seemed to be toward the good, she lifted her eyes to meet Carson's.

"Here's the deal," he began, "You get the high card, you win the goody box. I get the high card and you cook us a steak dinner. As a bonus, there's a spare room downstairs with a stout slide bolt on the door where you can bunk if you want."

One more expert riffle of the cards and she smacked the deck onto the table. Her poker face now in place, she nodded for Carson to make his cut.

He smiled and for a long beat savored her playing style. Then Carson snatched a quarter-inch stack from the deck and held it up confident this was going to be his lucky night.

The end.

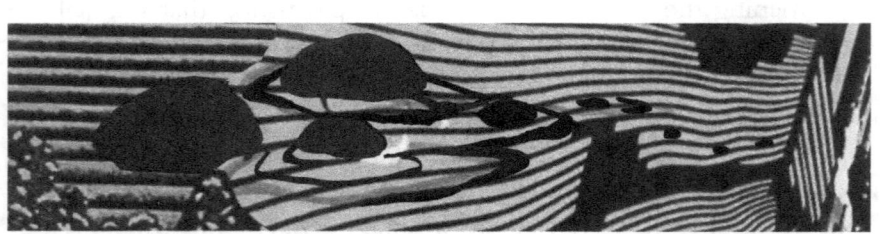

The Envelope

Don't keep looking at me like I'm stoned out of my head.

It wasn't my idea to leap before I looked, but what's an only child to do but toss caution to the wind? This whole misunderstanding wasn't my fault. I was just trying to be a good son but got lousy advice from my shrink and those crazy instructions my mother left me in a used envelope of all things. Can you imagine a wrinkled coffee-stained envelope causing all this trouble?

I'm freezing. Does this ambulance have a heater? Can I have a few more blankets? You know better than anyone I'm soaked to the bone from my accidental swim in the Chesapeake. In my condition I admit it was stupid of me to even think about walking out on those rocks slippery from the waves splashing on them.

But it was for my mother after all. True, I left her alone at the end of the jetty, but it was only for a few minutes. She was rock solid one second and then the next, floating away in the current like a loose buoy. Look, I don't expect a medal for trying to rescue her. After all, I'm her only living offspring. At least hear me out before jumping to conclusions, okay?

Thanks.

It happened like this . . .

. . . while the grains of sand in Mother's hourglass had just about drained to the bottom, I was trying my best to confront the issues my therapist said I needed to resolve before her time was up. If I didn't, he claimed I wouldn't grow as a person. I told him I was growing alright because I like to eat so much. The man has no humor, but I try.

Anyway, why now, you ask? It's simple: after all those false alarms, the doctors assured me this time Mother was dying and that was a stone-cold fact. As for coming to resolutions, it was "put up or shut up," and my therapist urged me to try and reach some sort of peace with the past while there was still time.

Being a member in good standing with the rescue squad, you must see certified basket cases every full moon. So you can testify that I'm no refugee from the lunar funny farm, though I do have a basketful of issues because Mother was a millstone for all my forty-nine years.

I should really shut up and let you attend to your professional duties. Can you possibly loosen the restraints? Unlike my mother, I'm not going anywhere. You can count on it.

I guess with this Bay Bridge traffic it'll take a while to get to the hospital. So, I might as well tell you some more, so you'll understand. I know I look a mess, soaked and shaking and all, but I'm okay, really.

I'm not the mechanical or athletic type, so things like wrenches, baseball, whatever, are Greek to me. In fact, I can't fix a thing on a car or even around the house. Orioles and Redskins? They're just birds and Indians to me. Give me Proust.

My mother had other ideas of what the all-American boy should be. She never let me forget it. Can you imagine being born a square peg in a world full of round holes?

No, probably not. You look like an all-American type. Don't get me wrong, I mean that in a positive way.

Unlike you, my thickheaded therapist refused to listen. Wait until he gets an earful about my mother's final outrage which, let me quickly say, has nothing to do with you or the good Kent Island rescue squad folks. Honestly, I count myself lucky to get this ride considering I don't have a job or insurance, nada, flat-out broke.

You can't imagine what it's been like to have a moron for a therapist, even if he is free, no thanks to Baltimore Family Services. I'll bet you've never had a minute of therapy? Well, I won't hold that against you.

That was a joke.

So anyway, in the last few sessions, from a whole laundry list, my therapist shopped for different stuff I could do to help me climb out of my rut. Therapy used to be almost enjoyable, just yakking for forty-five minutes on the taxpayer's dime. Then, all of a sudden, he wants me to dig deep and find these traumas that happened when I was this tall.

"We've just started scraping some dirt," the therapist said, "off the tip of a very big boulder."

That last session really rocked my foundation. It was a doozy and the 'homework' he had me do, as you now know, nearly got me drowned. Can you imagine being killed by your therapist? I would have had one hell of a lawsuit.

That was a joke.

If you hadn't fished me out of the Bay almost stone-cold dead, I wouldn't be here now to plead my case. Got any more blankets? My teeth are still clacking.

You're giving me that look, again. Dry clothes, some hot cocoa, and my keel will be even in no time.

But let me tell you what it's been like dealing with my mother and this crazy therapist, to boot. Having survived today's little setback, now I know I'm rock solid, stronger than anything they can dish out.

"Open up," my therapist had said, no beating around the bush, "you have to stop clinging to the past. You've hidden behind issues with your mother long enough." He thinks he's so superior sitting there in his big, black leather chair with all the answers, holding his coffee mug that says, "Kiss me, I'm bald."

"How?" I'd asked, feeling sick because the Italian hoagie suddenly wasn't agreeing with me so well. I do a lot of nervous eating and my diet and waistline have gone to hell. Come to think of it, maybe it's a good thing that I've got some extra body fat protecting me, right?

I guess you guys didn't find my glasses? I'm blind as a bat without them. I must've lost them jumping into the water. I'm a lousy swimmer and without my glasses it looked like Mother and I might be standing in front of the pearly gates together. That would have been Hell for sure.

That was a joke, kind of.

Where was I? Oh, yeah, so my therapist wasn't going to let me off the hook. He just blindly blundered headlong without any method to his meanness.

"Chip," he said, "we can sit here and do nothing or, and this is strictly up to you, we can devise a way for you to find some peace with your mother."

Well, for some reason it finally got to me. Up until then, I didn't believe her dying would happen anytime soon. Then, like turning on the light, I knew I'd better do something quick before her lamp went out.

"I've got it," I yelled. You should have seen. It nearly scared him half to death. "She's never said what she wants to do with her ashes. How about I find out and take care of it for her?"

Well, you'd think, by God, I'd struck gold. "Brilliant, absolutely brilliant," were his exact words. And then he babbled on about how I could use her passing as an opportunity to start the healing process. He said I could say all the things I couldn't while she was alive. I could mourn the loss of my childhood, and a bunch of other psychobabble. The man was manic. Almost gleeful. Maybe he needs a dose of his own therapy?

"For homework," the therapist said, "I want you to write down some things you've wanted to say to your mother but never have. No rules and don't show it to anybody. Read them to her while you're disposing of the ashes. Symbolically bury the hurtful past." Blah, blah!

While he was yakking away, I was thinking about how easy I was getting off. I could write some stuff, volumes actually. How complicated could it be? Read from the list like I was grocery shopping and then toss her ashes into the wind. Easy as pie.

What I didn't know was that pie was about to hit me full in the face, tossed by my own dear dead mother.

That's no joke.

Shortly after the session, I went to visit her bolstered with my new easy-peasy formula for creating a successful path at midlife. I said to her, "Mother, I think it's time we decided what you want done with your ashes." It came out just like I'd practiced. Good thing, since I almost laughed suddenly thinking she probably had a stash of butts and ashes hidden somewhere in her room. It's a miracle she hadn't blown up the place sneaking smokes with those oxygen tanks right next to her bed.

We'd never talked much once I was grown up. What with her bad health, no money and nearly deaf as a stone, she tended to be cranky and it was hard to have a civil word, truth to tell. Anyway, the long and the short of it was that someone had already written down her wishes back when she could talk better. So all I had to do was find the envelope with her instructions.

Boy, did I dread looking in those two large drawers of that bedside chest. It was the only hiding place in her room, and it's a wonder the drawers could still close with all those sugar, salt and pepper packets, wadded tissues, match books and paper scraps. Just like in her purse, bits of tobacco were stuck to everything.

Catholic pamphlets, I swear, filled half of one drawer. She was real devout until the boozing got out of hand after my little brother died and I was the only one left with her.

Well, I got to the bottom of things, so to speak, where important stuff would be hidden because anything valuable gets stolen. Would you believe I found a pint of whiskey, a little fake gold cross that I'd given her years ago, and two unopened packs of Kools? Those were always her favorite smokes. Finally, I spotted the envelope. It was re-used, you could tell because of the Shrine of St. Jude return address and some coffee mug rings.

Do Not Open until I'm gone was written on it like she was running away instead of dying. Now that I think on it, maybe it was just like her, always trying to get away but never able to hop off the treadmill.

What was there to say? I gave her a little peck on the cheek, took the envelope and went home to write all the wrongs done to me by my sweet little old mother.

Before I got back to visit she died and this made me a little sad because all we had was history and nothing else. Everything was handled businesslike over the phone. The only thing I had to do was schedule an appointment to pick up the ashes at the funeral home and read her instructions.

"HUMAN REMAINS," the orange and black label warned. Her ashes were packaged in a Styrofoam container no bigger than a small box of Kleenex, except sealed with plastic straps. Do you know how little of a life is left behind? And how light it was, just a handful of ashes, is all. Makes you think, now doesn't it?

For Mother's final instructions, I was hoping for something straightforward, you know, like scattering her ashes in a flower garden? Oh no, not my mother. Would you believe she wanted to be made into a "rock" and of all places, put out here on Kent Island on the Old Love Point jetty? A rock! Whatever happened to "ashes to ashes"? How was I, Mr. All Thumbs, supposed to make her into a rock? Only God can make a rock, right?

Being a local, I'm sure you've been to Old Love Point beach plenty of times. Probably drank beer and made out there when you were in high school? Ah, I see I'm right. Not much of a place, but my mother brought me there a few times when I was a kid. It was free and not that far from Baltimore. Guess she must've remembered it as a nice getaway.

Luckily, the rock part didn't turn out too bad. At Kent Island Hardware one of their sales guys, a real nice gentleman, was sympathetic and even offered to make the rock for me.

"Done a lot of fishing on the Bay," he told me, "They built the jetties on this island using concrete chunks from old highways. So, I figure a concrete rock will look right at home out there on the Point."

My usual totally helpless look must have played on him because he said, "We'll make it out back of the store on my lunch break."

The man was a wizard. In nothing flat he'd balled up chicken wire around the Styrofoam and glopped on some quick setting concrete he'd mixed from a bag and some water. Presto, he'd made a pretty decent rock. You'd hardly guess it was fake.

"This will fool anybody, guaranteed," he said, admiring his work.

"Is it heavy?" I asked, since I'm not in the best of shape. It looked sort of like a half-deflated concrete beach ball.

"Won't be too bad once it dries," he assured me, "'cause of the Styrofoam and ashes."

Sure enough, when I came back later, carrying it was a piece of cake though it felt a little stale because it was hard as a rock.

That was a joke.

Wouldn't you know the weather would be lousy today of all days. But it was too creepy having her around the house even if she did make a good doorstop.

That was a joke, the doorstop part. The creepy part was true.

Anyway, as I'm sure you probably know, walking out on that jetty is a real ankle buster. Not to mention the freezing rain and whipping wind. But my mind was made up.

"Okay, Mother, where?" I ask my mother, the rock, but the storm nearly tossed me into the Bay. Lucky klutz that I am, my tumble landed me smack between two big concrete chunks. My face almost went in the water but actually I was safe. But Mother did a humpy-dumpty and with no hardware clerk around I did my best to put her back together again. With cold Bay water lapping and slapping all the while, I got the pieces wedged into the jetty, though now it looked like a badly cracked dinosaur egg.

Talk about double dumb, here I'd risked life and limb and would likely get pneumonia only to reach inside my coat for the envelope with all my notes and come out empty handed. Well, I'm no good trying to remember things, so I had to go back to the car.

"Don't go anywhere," I told her, like I did the last few years whenever I'd take her out of the nursing home for a drive. She'd wait in the car while I went into the drugstore to get her Kools and a large bottle of mouthwash (twenty percent alcohol). She couldn't get around, even then, without a wheelchair. Even though I meant it as a joke, I was honest-to-God afraid she'd escape somehow, because she sure hated going back to that nursing home.

So, to retrieve my speech I had to leave her one last time in order to warm up some, then I could say my final words to dear old Mom. I don't know why I kept that unopened pint of whiskey from her drawer. I admit bringing it along was a big mistake except she always had a bottle stashed somewhere.

"To you, Mom, a real lady, tops in my book." I twisted off the cap and sipped, the car heater barely working. Geez, I'm not a drinker but somehow the pint got emptied in no time flat. Fortified, I grabbed my notes and the cheap little imitation gold cross ready to face the tempest.

The weather had gotten worse and the jetty even longer, not to mention more slippery. True, I was tipsy and I should have worn some sensible boots instead of cheap street shoes but, for Mother, I'd wanted to look nice at her sendoff.

So it took a while, but finally I made it out to the end and got situated to read my notes. The rain and spray had fogged up my glasses, so it took a minute before I realized.

She was gone.

That's no joke.

The wire-strapped Styrofoam box had somehow shed its cracked concrete shell. Honest-to-God it had set sail into the Bay and there I was, left with my unread notes looking on like it was a little lifeboat pushed along by the wind.

Anyway—hey, did you find my clothes? Before diving in to go after Mother I tore most of them off. I just now remembered. See, I'm not totally crazy after all.

Are we at the hospital?

* * *

Zipped up in their navy-blue nylon jackets emblazoned with school bus yellow patches, 'Kent Island Volunteer Rescue Squad,' two paramedics wheel the gurney into the emergency room.

"What you got?" the nurse says.

"Stable. Sound asleep. Hypothermia. Possible suicide," the driver answers. "Too cold for skinny-dipping."

"Any valuables?" the nurse asks.

"Not a stitch. A cheap little gold cross I had to pry out of his hand."

"I rode in back with him," says the other paramedic. "Jabbered the whole time, mostly incoherent. Totally stoned, said he was trying to rescue his mother. Said she was a rock."

"Well, this rock sure ain't feeling no pain," the nurse mutters scribbling notes, clipboard in hand.

"Must have been really rockin' and rollin'," the driver chuckles, "A swim in the bay on a day like today, you'd think he'd be stone cold sober!"

"Enough!" the nurse says holding up a hand. She laughs after a moment. "Roll him into three. Let's see if I have any success getting blood from a stone."

The end.

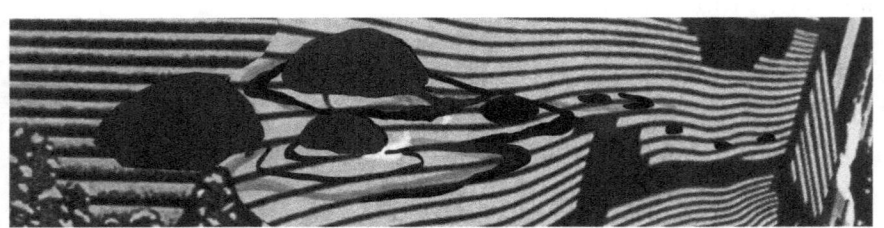

Maiden Flight Be Mine

"You got a clean knife?" Richard's voice was muffled by the back of his hand sliding under his nose. "Mine's got crap all over it." He held up a large hunting knife and then spit on the ground between his legs.

"You ain't messin' up my knife making your lunch," Doug said and took another drag on his cigarette. He eyed a raggedy wheelbarrow and decided that it was okay for a lunch seat.

After a few more puffs Doug flicked the butt toward a pile of mortar sand. He watched Richard make his lunch.

"Why don't you eat like a normal person?" he said pointing to his own black plastic lunch box and thermos.

Richard ignored the question and began making his sandwiches. Seated on an overturned bucket beside an old one-ton truck, he put three slices of bread on each thigh. With his finger he scooped some mayonnaise from the small jar onto the right-hand slices, then swirled each lump from the center of the bread out to the crust. He drew a smiley face on the third slice then sucked the excess mayonnaise from his finger.

For the left-hand slices he ripped chunks of tomato with his knife. He finished by moving two tomato pieces to the right making eyes for the smiley face. Richard wiped his knife and hands on his coveralls.

A warm September sun colored the West Virginia foothills with a faded orange haze and horseflies kept buzzing around the two men. A low rumble from heavy traffic over on the main road, Rt. 340, droned in the background. The journeymen bricklayers with their air-conditioned Chevy trucks had cruised into Charles Town for lunch. Richard and Doug, grunt laborers, stayed at the job site to eat and smoke away their lunch break.

"Almost got me some fresh pussy last night," Richard said as he assembled the sandwich halves, pressing them together until the soft bread was indented causing mayonnaise and tomato seeds to ooze up between his fingers.

"Close, huh?" Doug raised an eyebrow and tilted his head, "Who? That Darla girl with the two kids?"

The framing crew would be taking over in just a day or two, the huge foundation for the four-bedroom colonial style house they'd been working on needing only a couple more courses of cement block. Shovels, rakes, and hoes lay scattered around them like giant pick-up-sticks.

"Yeah, woulda' had some 'cept the damn boys came in from playin' outside just when I got my hand on the sweet thang." Richard eyed the other man over the top of his sandwich as he spoke. In a way, he thought, the best part of last evening was when they all bunched together on the sofa watching TV while sharing Cokes and jelly donuts.

"Her old man's still around, ain't he?" Doug asked.

"Comes by for Floyd, the oldest. He don't like taking Bud Junior 'cause he's a little slow; when he's got the kid he thinks people look at him funny." Richard got up, arched his back, stretched his arms over his head and grunted. "Least that's what Darla says. Bud Junior seems okay to me, 'course I'm use' to being around dimwits." He laughed until wracked by a fit of coughing.

Richard dug around for a pack of Marlboros from the pocket of his plaid work shirt that hung from the truck mirror. "Besides, she kind of said since they separated she don't put out no more for her old man."

"Want this last sandwich?" Richard asked through a blue cloud of smoke. "I ain't hungry no more." He squatted again on the bucket. Ashes sizzled in the lid of the mayonnaise jar as he tapped and rolled his cigarette on the rim.

"I can afford to eat normal," Doug said and added, "You could too if you'd keep that piece of crap running and made it to work half the time." He nodded toward Richard's '68 Ford Falcon that was jacked-up in the rear end exposing nearly bald racing tires. Doug leaned back into the wheelbarrow, pulled his baseball cap over his eyes and folded his arms across his chest.

"Gonna take it to the shop right after work," Richard said. "I borrowed a hundred from Daddy's money jar. The dumb shit won't miss it," he laughed.

"You still thinking about movin' out?" Doug asked, "'Bout time you took off on your own, ain't it?"

"I got a plan cookin' right now," Richard said with a big grin.

"The way you two drink and fight, you might as well be married to your Daddy." Doug lifted his cap and scratched his head, "If you was married you wouldn't have to pay rent."

"Wasn't so bad until he totaled his new Camaro. Only had the son-of-a-bitch four days and no insurance. Lost his license. He sits in front of the TV all day and his mind plays on him."

Doug sat up and said, "My maw was like that, watchin' the soap operas all damn day. I took off at sixteen and never looked back. Best thing I ever done."

"Just took off? Don't it make you kinda' sad, no family?" Richard asked.

"A man's gotta grow up sooner or later, be on his own," Doug said. He poured a cup of coffee from his thermos and looked at Richard. "So, when you gonna tell your old man to kiss your mother-fuckin' ass?"

Richard picked at some small lumps of dried mortar stuck to his coveralls. "Soon as I see if Darla's any good. Even if it ain't the best pussy in the world, she's got other things . . . I could be real cozy there just shackin' up."

"Have you lost your friggin' mind? Don't be a fuckin' asshole." Doug moaned and tipped his cap back. "I don't care what she said. If she's getting that support check, he's porkin' her." Doug snorted like a pig.

"How'd you like your nuts put in our watch pocket?" Veins stood out on Richard's head and his ears turned deep red. He picked up a long-handled shovel and started toward the other man. Doug scrambled out of the wheelbarrow tipping it over, and yanked a hammer from the loop on his tool belt.

"Look man. Take it easy," he shouted, reflexively crouching in a fighting stance. Waving the hammer menacingly, he yelled, "I'm just trying to talk sense. You can wet your dick without moving in. Come on, man, cool it. Just cool it."

Richard stopped. He stood motionless for a few moments, then dropped the shovel and leaned against the truck, tilting his head toward the sky and closing his eyes.

"I can't stand livin' with Daddy no more; I need some room." Richard's mouth opened wide to fill his lungs. A small curved gap showed where half a tooth was missing. He held his chest full of air then let it ease out slowly.

"Ever just want to close your eyes and have everything be different?"

"Yeah, I guess so," Doug said warily but wasn't ready to let go of the hammer just yet.

"I do." Richard inhaled deeply again, his eyes still closed and added, "All the time."

"Come on, Richard," Darla said, "you gotta stop treating him like he was normal. You know Bud Junior ain't right." She picked up the quiet child and carried him to the boys' bedroom at the other end of the trailer. The old catcher's mitt and the new baseball Richard had brought lay on the sofa next to a half slice of white bread smeared with grape jelly.

Darla returned and busied herself picking up dirty clothes and dishes scattered about the cramped living room. "Didn't expect nobody or I'd a straightened up a little," she said to no one in particular and then looped an oily strand of black hair behind her ear.

"Yeah, well, I thought I'd stop by and give Bud Junior his presents," Richard said dejectedly. "Didn't mean no harm." Appearing taller than his six feet because of the low ceiling in the trailer, he waited fidgeting, chewing his fingernails

Darla stopped rearranging the laundry and dirty dishes and laid her hands on her wide hips. "You just don't understand. He ain't never gonna be normal. Just leave him be." She brought her hands together like she was praying and said, "I thank the Lord I got one that's all right."

"Look, he's just a little slow, that's all," Richard pleaded. "Besides, I was slow and I turned out all right, didn't I?"

Darla ignored him as she went back to straightening. There were piles of magazines, romance novels and bric-a-brac to be sorted, dusted and arranged. She tugged back the baggy sleeves of her yellow and green kimono before attacking each mound.

"Now that the car's running good, I ain't missed a day's work this week." Richard spoke softly, stepping lightly on the rusty orange shag carpet as he angled toward the woman. She was busy in the corner of the room next to the green vinyl easy chair and pecan coffee table.

Richard moved up behind Darla and stared down at the top of her head. Tiny white specks dotted the mat of black hair. He put both of his callused hands firmly on her shoulders, afraid she'd move away.

His breath came in quick gasps as his excitement raced ahead of his maneuvering. God, he marveled silently at his good fortune, I'm finally going to have her.

Darla stood still as a post as he pulled the silky kimono up to the middle of her back. He took a quick look down at the spotted, dimpled ass and the thick folds of skin that stuck out at her waist. Love handles, he thought to himself. He fumbled at his fly, undoing his dirty work pants and tugging at his boxer shorts until they dropped to his ankles.

"Uh, man this is nice," he whispered, "I like a big woman." Richard kneaded and squeezed the doughy white flesh around her middle and rocked back and forth on his heels. After a few minutes he finished with a weak grunt.

"Jesus, Darla, that was the best I've ever had. No kidding." Richard took a last look at Darla's reddened, dimpled skin, then let her gown fall.

"It was okay, I guess," she said flatly starting again with her cleaning.

"I was hoping I could move in here," Richard said, his words fluttering with nervousness.

Darla began turning and suddenly he dipped to tug frantically at his shorts and pants tangled in a knot around his knees. He straightened mortified, worried about being exposed to this woman for the first time, his manhood shriveled, hiding like a startled box turtle. Unable to meet her gaze, he focused on a wall poster of Jesus watching over a sleeping child taped to the dark paneling behind her, hoping she wouldn't look down at his shrunken privates. Please Lord, he pleaded silently, anything but that.

"Here?" Darla asked, her voice flat.

"Yes," Richard croaked, his chest heaving, "We could be uh, a . . .

family like, you know . . . the kids . . . trailer." He swallowed the pleading that would come out if he continued.

"You gotta leave for a while," Darla said smoothing her kimono, "My husband'll be here soon to drop off Floyd. You can come back later after he's gone, if you feel like it."

"Good, nobody's here," Richard mumbled as he wheeled his car sharply to the left after crossing the bridge and creeping down the steep hill to a flat gravel-covered clearing. It was an isolated spot backed up against the stone outcroppings of the Blue Ridge with the Shenandoah River close enough to hit with a skipping stone. He'd brought a six-pack of Stroh's to wait for the evening to pass and Darla's husband to leave.

Not bad. He thought about the dates they'd had since meeting— the groping and teasing and the kids always bustin' in at the wrong times. Now I've had her, she's mine. God, that was some fine pussy. He was grinning from ear to ear at the thought.

The cool of early evening created a heavy mist as it settled on top of the wide, lazy river with the days still being hot in late September. Richard thought back to the first time he'd brought Darla and the kids here after they had hit it off so well at the Charles Town bowling alley. The smothering heat and humidity of July was at its height bringing out enough townies to crowd the spit of land. He and Darla had sat on the hood of the car sipping beer and watching the river like everybody else. They made the kids stay inside the car because of the broken glass, crushed cans and other trash tossed from parked cars.

In the early hours of the morning, after that night of jabbering, the kids finally huddled asleep in the back seat and most of the noisy crowd gone, Richard had got up the nerve to kiss Darla. That was the moment he had first felt the vague unsettling change: a sort of push, a shedding of something and then a faint glimmering of something else. Each meeting with Darla after that made the gnawing in his gut a little sharper but he couldn't figure it out any clearer.

Now, careful to park in the same spot, he twisted the cap off another beer and sighed. "What a roll," he thought, "No missed work days, car running great, and now I'll have a girl of my own. I can tell my old man to kiss off for good."

Richard flicked the cap out the window. A loud rustling followed by a rapid beating and a screech roared nearby out of the shadows.

"Shee-it!" Richard dropped away from the window throwing his hands up for protection, while beer foam squirted out of the mouth of the bottle drenching his pants.

"Fuckin' bird," he hissed, his heart still thumping against his windpipe. "Like to give me a heart attack." The ca-chirring beat of the air diminished in the distance leaving only a mute darkness. Richard slowly sat up. The quiet that followed rattled him and set him to thinking about something, anything, to fill up the emptiness.

First, he thought about screwing Darla but his mind kept seeing the trailer all jammed full of crap—toys scattered over every inch of carpet, magazines and junk piled everywhere with no room for anything else.

"Shee-it!" Richard hissed when he pictured Darla knocked-up, growing bigger and bigger. Then there would be no room for him.

"Damn, damn, damn," he murmured, shaking his head slowly, trying to think of something else.

A picture of his father came to mind. If I move out, he thought, then who'll keep an eye on the old man when he gets stinkin' drunk? Who'll watch the Redskins games with him on the stupid little black and white TV with the snowy picture? Or listen to the Orioles games on the radio, then pick all the damn peanut shells up off the rug?

In his mind Richard could see his father's crabbed hands making a swim stroke in the air as he retold war stories. There was one about wading ashore on the coral reef and hearing his best buddy scream and pitch forward into the Pacific surf and all the olive-green helmets bobbing in the bloody salt water.

You could almost smell the smoking, spinning tires every time the old man bragged about his '56 Chevy coupe. There was his father tottering on the edge of a chair in the kitchen, popping the clutch and banging the gears, showing how he'd whipped everybody's ass that long, dry summer in 1959. "It was a runnin' machine," he'd say again and again between sips of beer. And then he would lament again how after his summer of victories he'd rolled it down the mountainside that winter and he was laid-up in the hospital three weeks and how his leg never healed right.

"Damn doctors, anyway. I use' to be a hell of a carpenter." How many times had Daddy said that?

"I've got to have my own life. Let the old fart find somebody else to hang on to." Richard opened another beer and growled at the windshield. Then he thought about going back to Darla's later after her old man cleared out and pulling up her green kimono again. He wouldn't leave. Just flat out say, "I'm stayin'."

Except what if her husband gets real comfortable and spends the night and don't leave? Ever.

Richard frantically tossed the empties out the window. The sound of exploding beer bottles echoed off the rock outcroppings.

"Gotta get there and make sure that don't happen." Richard fumbled with the keys until he found the ignition, hit the gas pedal twice and turned the key, *Click, click, click, click.*

"Fuckin' battery!" He shouted and pounded on the steering wheel until his fists hurt too much and then added weakly, "Just when everything was going my way."

He sat for a while, his anger slowly draining. Reaching for another beer, he saw little Bud's present on the seat. The mitt had been his own, a surprise to him from his daddy on the first warm day of spring when he was six years old. Almost every evening that summer they tossed a ball back and forth in the small open area of patchy grass in the center of the trailer court.

Twice that summer they'd made the long trip to Baltimore and sat in the bleachers all Sunday afternoon and watched the Orioles play doubleheaders. Daddy got two bags of dark roasted peanuts and three cups of beer. Richard had a cotton candy and two fat hot dogs with onions and lots of mustard.

He cracked a grin as he felt his mouth watering and longed for those bright sunny days down in Baltimore with pennants snapping in the breeze and the crackle of peanut shells underfoot on the concrete steps of Memorial Stadium. It all seemed so long ago and out of reach.

Another memory crowded in on him. He could almost feel his father's trembling shoulders, drunk and crying while he relived the memory of getting home late after a double shift to find the tuna casserole in the oven still warm; his wife, Mona, left him for good. Richard was in the crib on his stomach sound asleep on freshly laundered sheets. It'd always been just him and Daddy and sad drunken stories about a woman Richard couldn't picture.

Maybe Doug was right, Richard thought. Maybe I was getting a little pussy crazy.

Richard picked up the mitt and the last two beers and started walking toward Rt. 9. With any luck, he thought, I'll hitch a ride to town in time to listen to the second game of the doubleheader with Daddy.

Light's on in Daddy's room so the Orioles must still be playing, Richard thought as he kicked through the high grass surrounding the house after thumbing a ride from the river. The beer long gone, he clutched the old catcher's mitt tightly to his chest for warmth and because he was happy.

"What the fuck?" Richard tried the door. It was never locked before that he could remember and he didn't have a key. The faint sound of an excited announcer's voice meant the Orioles were probably doing something good.

Taped to the door was a piece of paper. Richard pulled it off and stepped back to catch the light coming from the upstairs window.

godam thef com cler yur shit out a hear in the mornin im dun with you, he could just make out.

Richard sat down on the step, knees and hands shaking. Putting the note aside, his hand trembling, he fumbled to get the catcher's mitt on trying to reclaim the feeling that had drawn him back here. He thought hard about what had happened recently between him and Darla, with his daddy, and with Doug. None of it made any sense except that each had something he wanted. Closing his eyes and inhaling deeply, he slowly made up a new wish; one big enough for all his new dreams.

"I wish that everything could be different and the same."

Grabbing hold at least to this fleeting grasp, some of the heaviness lifted. Richard picked up the paper squinting to see in the dim light, just as Daddy must have rolled onto his side to go to sleep, turning off his bedside lamp.

As his usual habit, the radio remained on and the reassuring sound of the announcer's voice over the din of the crowd noise meant the game still wasn't over.

The end.

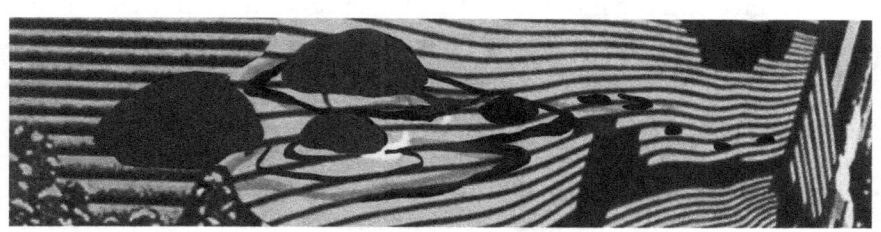

I Want Candy

"I'm tellin' you it's got everything! And I mean *EVERYTHING*."
Darryl was trying to 'b.s.' me into buying this dirty book for us.
"And," he rushed on, "I saw it on the drugstore bookrack just yesterday, so it's got to be there."

"Why didn't YOU buy it?" I asked the lame-brain.

"Are you nuts?" he shot back. "You look older and nobody'd say a thing to you."

Standing a little taller, I asked, "What's it called?"

"*Candy*, is what I think I heard."

"You're a knucklehead if you can't remember one word," I practically yelled.

Darryl spent half his life secretly listening in on his older brother and his hoodlum friends. If they ever caught him, he'd get punched-out because they rode motorcycles, had ducktail haircuts, smoked Luckies and hung out in a crappy garage behind Darryl's house. No dumb little punks allowed.

He finally looked at me, smiling his toothy smile and said, "Candy is dandy! It's *Candy* for sure."

Hopping from one foot to the other, I knew he was ready to explode. When he couldn't keep his yap shut for another second he squeaked, "The book is *FULL* of fantastic stuff. It's all about girls and everything."

That was hard to believe. But I was desperate too. "You mean how they do it?"

"*Yeah!*" he shouted, "That's what I've been trying to tell you. *Christ*, I'll even give you the money!" He fished around in his pockets, finally pulling out a wrinkled dollar bill and some sweaty change. He shoved the bill and coins at me and like my little league coach, said, "I know you can do it."

That was yesterday. It took me all night and all day today to stop shaking when I thought about the secret mission.

This is today, and the last time Darryl's going to get me to do his dirty work. No way I won't get caught and be grounded for the rest of my life. The drugstore is usually my favorite place to hang out on the way home from school. There's a U-TEST-IT-FREE tube tester just inside the door. I find old TV's and radios that have been trashed since they don't work anymore. I use the tester to see if any of the tubes are still good and I replace the bad ones. That usually fixes them right up. If a buddy is looking for a TV or a radio for their hangout, they know to come to me. So most times a few tubes are always clinking in my pocket like right now. This'll help if a sales lady asks me what I'm doing hanging around.

Mel throws away a lot of good stuff that I scrounge for parts. He runs the Radio and TV Repair next to the sub shop, two doors up from the drugstore. Sometimes I get old tubes out of the big dumpster behind Mel's. On my way to the drugstore, I checked and there was a big old radio with the back already off and all I had to do was grab a few of the tubes.

Right inside the drugstore, I spot the cashier behind the checkout counter flipping through a magazine probably about movie stars or detective stories with a bug-eyed woman tied up and gagged on the cover. With one eye on her, I make my way to the round wire rack of paperback books near the magazine stand. I don't want her getting suspicious, so I pretend to be real interested in things like I'm going to buy something.

Half my life is spent around this shopping center. Every day I plunk a newspaper on the counter of the sub shop and if the owner,

Phil, isn't too busy cooking he gives me a wave. This is my delivery territory. Each afternoon I deliver the Baltimore *Evening Sun* to the apartments nearby. "Light for All," is the paper's motto and now when it gets dark early, I wish it were really true.

I want to listen to England, Russia, and places like that but you need a short-wave radio to listen to stations that far away. I got a book last year, *Build Your Own Short-Wave Radio for Under $10*, and have been dreaming about it ever since. Nothing's better than messing around with vacuum tubes and fixing up radios and TVs.

Unless it's getting a good look at the pages of *Candy*.

The cashier lady coughs and I jump about ten feet before I remember I haven't done anything yet. Sneaking a look, I don't think she can see me behind the bookrack. Outside the store, Darryl's probably dodging back and forth wondering what's taking so long and stopping every so often to spy through the Halloween witches, corn stalks, ghosts and all the other crap in the front window display. Tough nuggies, he can freeze his butt off, since he was too chicken to buy . . . THE BOOK.

It's hard for me to believe that this little book could change everything but my you-know-what certainly thinks so and is constantly popping up at the worst possible times. It really seems to have a mind all its own.

Just to make it look like I'm shopping, I grab *Football Facts, 1960*, off the rack and flip the pages. I hate football but act real interested in case somebody asks what I'm doing. I'll say, "Checking on Johnny Unitas," and give them a "Go Colts," for good measure. The rack moves a little with each nudge of my foot. Finally, after about a week, I spot IT near the bottom. Slowly, I put the football book back and kneel down like I'm going to tie my high tops while eyeing the pink cover with black letters, *CANDY*. There's only the one copy, so this is it or nothing. My chest heaves like I've been running a million miles.

Retying my sneaker for good measure, I take one last look toward the front counter to see if anyone is in line. You can't be too careful because some friend of my mother's might be here getting some toothpaste or aspirin. You never know.

"Can I help you, young man?" a woman asks from behind me.

"Oh, crap!" I say accidentally, and even though it really isn't a cuss word, I know adults don't like that word. Caught red-handed peeking at a dirty book, I'm dead for sure and stand up straight hoping my posture will save the day.

"Excuse me?" the sales lady asks, but her voice and look tell me she didn't really hear.

"Tubes," I answer pulling out a handful to show them as evidence. "My sick grandmother's TV is on the fritz, and I came here to test the tubes." I add, "She really misses her soap operas."

Hearing me just fine, she says, "What a nice young man. Not one of those juvenile delinquents." Spinning on her heels, she heads toward the back of the store, where the pharmacist waits behind a tall counter like he's the king.

Wait. If I can see him, can he see me? Maybe he told that sales lady to spy on me, but she saw I wasn't doing anything. It's not like I can get arrested if I'm going to pay, right?

Taking a deep breath, keeping my head down the whole time, I snatch the book, charge to the checkout counter and fork over the money. In less than thirty seconds I'm out the door into the cold night air.

Darryl hops up from his seat on the curb and is all over me like a big, stupid mutt.

"Let me see!" Darryl squeaks, cold puffs follow each word and the spiky front of his crew-cut stands up like he just got electrocuted. Jumping from one foot to the other, he keeps grabbing and shouting, *"You got it, you got it!"*

All of a sudden, I don't care about the book so much and would rather be home with the smell of sauerkraut and pork roasting in the oven and fighting with my brothers and sisters over the TV.

"Yeah, dummy," I say. "You think I bought an empty bag?" I hold it tightly to my chest for no reason I can think of.

"Lemme see," he says, fingers twitching like he can't wait another minute to get his hands on the prize.

"No!" I say. "We gotta hide it."

"Why?" Darryl shouts back over the roar of cars whizzing by on Edmondson Avenue blasting us with leaves and trash.

For a second I didn't have an answer and wanted to keep the book closed for now. Finally I say, "It's dark and we're late getting home. If we start reading about how girls do it we won't want to stop."

Darryl looks like he's ready to cry. "Just let me see the cover for criminy sakes."

"No," I say firmly like my father, and take a step back to be out of his reach. "We gotta hide it for tonight. Some place nobody would think of looking."

"Where?" Darryl asks and looks puzzled like he's in math class.

We both stand there and I'm starting to feel stupid with Darryl staring bug-eyed when it hits me. "We'll stash it in the dumpster behind Mel's." I know it doesn't get picked up until tomorrow afternoon because that's when I check to get the most stuff.

"Yeah! Cool." Darryl cheers up. "We can read it before school and brag all day."

Dinner lasts forever. I answer the usual questions between mouthfuls of pork and kraut. Nothing happened at school and I failed only one quiz. Everybody except me talks in slow motion.

Then I wash piles of dishes and get no help from my older sister, only grief.

"This plate is dirty." Mary points to an invisible speck. "Wash it again." She won't dry anything unless it's spotless.

Homework takes a century. And it's all the subjects I hate: math, English, history, and science.

Bedtime at last and all I can do is toss and turn in the darkness. Pictures of girls I know float above me on the ceiling: my sisters, girls at school, girls on my paper route, even women like my mother. None of them give me a clue or even a hint of the stuff they're supposed to do. Nothing. I can't even picture a girl without clothes, let alone naked in the same room with me.

It's like they have a big secret that I'm not supposed to know about until I get married, or worse, I'll find out when I'm old and don't care anymore. But I know *some* things, clues actually. My friend, Sam, told me a while ago. It didn't make too much sense and I thought he might be pulling my leg.

"Big ones," he'd said. "Like two great big vanilla ice cream cones with a cherry on top of each one." He was cross-eyed looking down at his hands cupped a few inches from his chest.

"You lick each one," Sam said, closing his eyes and lapping like a thirsty dog licking first at one hand then the other. He licked and licked until all the pretend ice cream was gone.

"Yeah?" I questioned him and wet my lips. Sam talked as if it was like having the best dessert of your whole life before the greatest dinner of your whole life. It was hard to imagine something better than a rare, charcoal broiled steak smothered in fried onions with a pile of mashed potatoes loaded with Land O'Lakes butter followed by a big slice of chocolate cake topped with two scoops of butter brickle ice cream.

Sam must have seen my look and said, "I can't be tellin' you every-thing. You're too young and it'll drive you crazy. No sir." He shook his head emphatically so I'd get the message.

This confounded me. "YOU'RE not crazy, are you?"

"I'm different." Sam smiled. "Because I'm sixteen and you're a kid."

Ice cream was all I learned from Sam and already I liked it. "Tomor-row," I swore in the stillness of my dark bedroom, "The BOOK will tell me how it's done and I'll know more than all the guys at school."

My lungs were about to burst as I rounded the corner to the alley behind Mel's. I'd planned to get up extra early and b.s.'d my mother about joining a study club at school. I musta slept through the alarm but raced through a bowl of cornflakes only to get slowed down hav-ing to stuff extra books in my book bag so my mother wouldn't get suspicious about study club.

"Jesus, I thought you'd never get here," Darryl said. He sat on the curb near the big green dumpster, his hands stuck between his knees. "One more minute and I'd of gotten the book myself," he proclaimed, like he was hot stuff.

"Well, I'm here." I heaved trying to catch my breath. The dump-ster looked huge and solid, the perfect place to stash our prize. Darryl hopped up and scurried over next to me, getting way too close.

"*Back off,*" I yelled, and shoved him.

Like a rubber band, he bounced right back ready to dive in.

"Wait you idiot." I held out my arm to block him. "We gotta think on this."

"What?" Darryl asked, his eyes ready to pop out of his head. He was sweating.

"I got to thinking last night," I started to say.

"Thinking?" Darryl stared, like I was a mental case.

I held up a hand to shut him up. "What if it will show that we're . . . we're finally men?" I'd worried that I might start looking at girls and women differently, and somebody like my mother would notice.

"That's the whole point, you moron," Darryl shouted, his spiky hair even spikier. "Don't you want to be a man?"

He was right, but I had to act like this was a big decision only I could make.

"You chicken or what?" he razzed me, and I was about to shove him again.

But we both froze, first feeling the vibration through our sneakers and then the low rumble. From nearby, an alley or two away we heard the *clang, crunch* and *pop* of a garbage truck making the early morning rounds. A man angrily shouted something, but it was drowned out by the *beep, beep, beep* of a truck backing away from an emptied dumpster.

"*Noooo!*" we howled into the sharp October dawn just giving way to daylight.

I tagged the dumpster first, put a foot on the side brace and pulled myself up like the practiced move it was. It took two hands to release the latch to the side door and I jumped down to let it swing open. The door moved as fast as cold molasses and took about an hour to bang against the side. Stretching with both hands, I grabbed the open frame and pulled up struggling to get against the slippery side with my clumsy feet. Finally, my hands hurting like crazy, I was staring into the dark opening, while the *chuga-chuga-chuga* of the trash truck died away.

"*Can you see it?*" Darryl yelled, the sound of his big feet making hopping noises like a bouncing rabbit.

"Crap," I said back to him, and he knew what I meant. A bunch of sparkling tubes were still in the bottom corner and I almost crawled in to get them.

"Crap," I said again and jumped down next to Darryl.

"Jeez," Darryl kicked the dumpster, "How are we ever going to learn anything?"

"Don't know," I answered shaking my head.

We picked up our book bags and headed slowly toward Rock Glen Junior High for another dumb day at school.

The end.

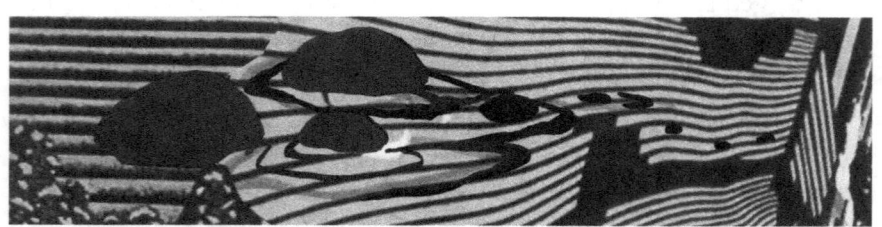

Small Craft Warnings
(or The Envelope Revisited)

They rested in a Styrofoam package about the size of a small loaf of bread on the passenger's seat of the old Chevy. Her ashes. There was a metal tag with her name imprinted on it and in red it was labeled, "Human Remains." Jim had handled the package gingerly, surprised by how little was left of a life that lasted seventy-three years.

Until that moment he'd waited to open the envelope containing his mother's final instructions. The handwriting was neat so a nurse or orderly must have written it for her. After reading the first part he was relieved. She wanted her ashes to be placed at the end of the jetty at Old Love Point Park. He remembered the park fondly. It was about an hour's drive, just across the Chesapeake Bay Bridge. When his mother wanted to get away from Baltimore's summer heat, they'd pack a picnic and bathing suits and spend a lazy day at the shore.

But the second part caused him some uneasiness. She wanted her ashes made into a rock? He read it a second time to be sure she meant *a rock*. As to what shape or size or even the material to be used was left for him to devise. He wasn't handy with tools and his mother had always considered this one of his many failings as a son. Maybe this was her way of giving him one last chance to measure up.

It was early November, about fifty degrees, and spitting rain as Jim drove to the shore. The wind was gusting and the sky an endless sheet of gray. Small craft warnings would have been issued keeping recreational boaters off the water. Too bad. While sunbathing he remembered they'd made a game of counting sailboats. Powered by improbably large, colorful sails, boats had skimmed over the water, tilted so much he was sure they'd topple into the white-capped waves. He'd miss that and the other silly games she'd make up to entertain him when he was little.

He looked over at the passenger seat where she should have been sitting, buckled in, not in the present form she now took.

With the help of a Home Depot salesclerk, the rock had turned out okay. He'd taken pity on Jim and used his lunch hour to help. Mashing chicken wire into a vaguely round shape made a ball-like form. Then in a plastic pail, they mixed her ashes with some quick setting concrete and enough water to make a thick paste. They slathered and patted the mixture over the wire form until it looked like a lumpy soccer ball. Given that the core was mostly air trapped inside the hollow mesh, once it dried it weighed only a few pounds. But it looked enough like a rock to pass muster with the clerk, and Jim let out a sigh of relief. With that chore behind him, fulfilling his mother's final wish would be a snap, or so he hoped.

In a cardboard box, the rock sat buckled into the passenger's seat next to him just like Mother had so many times. Every Saturday for the past six years, he'd take her out from the nursing home for the day, driving around Baltimore as she reminisced about the old days. Thinking of this reminded him of her chatter, which he'd learned to mostly ignore long, long ago. But now he would have welcomed some sound, even the familiar ramblings of her raspy-voice.

Also laying on the seat was his folded handwritten list of things he wanted to say to his mother but could never muster the courage. His therapist said it would be cathartic and, after some gentle prodding, Jim agreed so long as he could really speak his mind. Her drinking, frequent moves to cheaper and cheaper apartments, unreliable male companionship and other indignities had been a constant source of embarrassment and worry.

"There are no rules," the therapist had advised, "Just go with your feelings."

The park looked abandoned and nothing like he remembered. Then again, it had been well over thirty years since his last visit. There were a few picnic tables that had seen better days and two forlorn swing sets. It was raining just enough to keep the wipers on and Jim shivered and hugged himself for warmth. The jetty stretched far out into the choppy water.

As he made his way across the gravel lot to the thin beach and jetty, his hat sailed away and the rock turned ice cold, freezing his hands. He'd forgotten to bring gloves and even with the wool overcoat he'd buttoned to the neck, the wind was piercing.

The jetty was constructed from chunky rocks and broken slabs of concrete with stubby, rusted iron bars protruding from them. He figured it was debris from some long-ago highway project. The jumbled mess was heavily matted in places with what looked like slimy green shag carpet. It looked dangerous. Threatening.

"Thanks a lot, Mom," he muttered, carefully inching his way to the end of the jetty. It seemed to take a long long time. Waves were breaking and splashing up in white foam and, at the water's edge, he nearly fell trying to place the rock where the waves couldn't take it. Breakers smashed into the jumbled slabs and rocks, soaking his loafers. By then, he didn't care and wanted to be dry and warm as soon as possible.

Mission accomplished, he thought.

Then he swore inside his head, remembering—the damn list was still in the car.

"Don't go anywhere," he said to the rock, recalling other trips with his mother once she'd entered the nursing home. He'd take her out to buy her cigarettes, leaving the motor running. "Don't go anywhere," he'd say, knowing how much she hated going back each time. In the back of his mind, he wished one day he'd come out of the 7-11 to see her tearing down the highway to some faraway place where she'd be happy.

Now, he couldn't even wish for her escape.

Without having to lug the rock, it was a little easier clambering over the jagged chunks and slopes back to the car. Once inside the old Chevy, the anemic heater barely cut the chill. His glasses needed cleaning and his nose dripped. Searching the glove compartment for some tissues, he found the pint. From her belongings at the nursing home it was the only thing he'd saved. She'd always had a bottle stashed somewhere nearby. Having it stowed in the glove compartment seemed fitting.

"To you, Mom." Twisting off the cap he took a sip. The whiskey tasted good, even if it was cheap, and he could feel the warmth spreading from his belly to his frozen limbs. The radio didn't work and there was nothing to do but swig, try not to think about what he had to do, though he already half-knew, and stare at the endless horizon.

Even with all the animosity and hurt, at least she had always been there. Someone, rather than no one.

Now, alone, totally alone, he couldn't keep from dwelling on his own horizons. What lay behind and what before him. Behind were the failures—a marriage that didn't work out, college never completed, a career that he'd walked away from. He might have done things differently and hadn't. Just like his mother, he mused. Then there was the horizon ahead—an endless monotony, like the tide coming in and going out, coming in and going out.

He swigged again. And again. Seated in the car, he tried to muster the courage for what he had to do next, feeling a warmth and light-headedness coming over him.

He rarely drank, and now he wondered why not.

Why not? He shouted inside his head.

After draining the bottle, he tried to remember if he'd passed any liquor stores nearby. None came to mind and the thought of going back out in the cold seemed daunting now that he had a snoot full of booze and was beginning to feel vaguely human. That is, if humans felt the acute surges that were loosed within him now. He considered just driving away and leaving things as they were.

No. This wouldn't be right.

The hard knot of resentment and a tangle of other, unnamable feelings that had awakened in his gut wouldn't let him.

Yes. This is what he'd come here to finish. He gathered up the forgotten pages containing his list of grievances, tucked them safely inside his coat and pushed open the balky car door.

Loosened by the whiskey, surges of conflicting emotion flooded through his chest. Grief crashing into relief. Resentment slamming into longing, and the wish that he could just let it all go.

The wind had kicked-up even more and the rain came down in cold sheets and the tilted concrete had gotten more slippery and the twisted metal rods more menacing.

Small crafts be warned! Jim bellowed, creeping crab-like, imagining he was a lone sailor navigating a treacherous sea, not unlike the way he'd felt since childhood.

At the point, Jim stood as straight as he could on whiskey legs and the uneven surfaces. His list fluttered in the wind as he tried to read it through wet bifocals. Several attempts to clean his glasses failed and he gave up reading. Two of the pages slipped out of his wet fingers and disappeared in the churning waves.

Memory would have to do, as he tried to recall all the angry things he'd carefully composed. Swaying in the buffeting wind and spray, a different sort of recollection came to mind. He remembered his mother reading, *Mike, the Steam Shovel*, and he'd begged her to read it again and again until he fell asleep.

Balling-up the last soggy page in his fist, Jim acknowledged defeat. The cold, wind and alcohol infusion had exhausted him and he couldn't summon up anger anymore. It was time to leave, and he wanted one last look at the lumpy rock to fix it in his mind.

Nothing lay at his feet.

The grayish orb had slipped into the Chesabeake Bay, bobbing in the water, already some distance away driven along by the wind. The hollow core must have given it buoyancy like a beach ball, and off his mother went.

Come back! he shouted instinctively, motioning frantically.

Who was he calling to? The stone? The ashes? The mother who had abandoned him for whiskey and a trail of losers?

Leaving me again? he screamed.

Maybe the slab wobbled. Maybe it had become slicker from the surf and sea slime. Or maybe without thinking he jumped, but . . . mid-plunge he realized he was headed into the icy Bay.

Splashing and kicking, spluttering saltwater he was able to achieve a floating position on his back. There were panicked shouts from the shore, but he'd lost his glasses and wasn't able to see who it was.

What became clear was the horizon ahead. One he'd somehow always known he would set out for one day.

Oddly, the water didn't seem that cold after the initial shock, and he began to feel comfortable. Even warm.

He rolled onto his stomach and swam until he caught up with the fleeing rock. Cradling it against himself, fueled with liquid courage and resignation, Jim used his other arm and feet for propulsion. Moving steadily away from shore, he slurred, "Let's go to someplace sunny and warm."

The end.

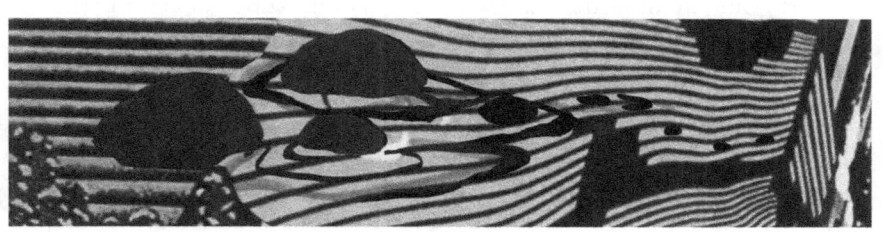

The River Stories
Part One: Carry Me to the River

In the bright starlight a fat possum waddled across the path, not looking at Fishy. Ordinarily he'd have trailed after it, but not this October night. "Go on, git," he hissed softly. The critter waggled away rustling through the scrubby grass.

"Could be de devil tryin' to snatch a spirit," Fishy cautioned himself.

Resettling the digging pick on his shoulder, he cocked an ear listening for anyone else afoot. A slave creepin' in the dark would spook any white folk and he'd surely get a whippin'. The thought brought a slight smile to his lean stubbly face, an old bag of bones like himself putting the fear of God in white folks. They are right skittish lately since Mr. Lincoln might get elected.

All was quiet so he snatched up the gunny sack and continued. In a short while he turned from the footpath and felt his way slowly cross-country down the steep grade, slipping between spindly trees and stepping around rock outcroppings. It was familiar ground where he knew he wouldn't pass any houses with dogs tied up in the yard or slinking under a porch.

At the bottom of the hill he stopped again to listen. This being Sunday night, the sprawling brick U.S. Armory buildings to his right were quiet. A little farther downriver, several lights flickered in the lower town of Harpers Ferry while faint voices floated on the crisp night air. The B&O train depot, telegraph office and hotel had people coming and going at all hours. Lately town folk had started carrying pistols and rifles patrolling for slaves and free blacks out at night when they shouldn't be. Unless a white man was attending, black folks couldn't even have their own church service.

"We's almos' der," he whispered to the sack. Directly across a flat stretch of ground, a canal blocked his way. It was a man-made sluice to divert river water for powering the Armory machinery. "Don' be skert," he added, hefting the sack high in the air overhead then, with one long stride, he lunged hip deep into cold dark water. Pushing forward and swinging his upper body side to side, he quickly crossed.

One of his shoes was lost to the bottom muck, and his pants would take half the night to dry in the cool autumn air. Luckily his thin jacket and shirt remained mostly dry. Lowering the sack and shifting the pick on his shoulder, Fishy stepped lightly across the railroad tracks, favoring his one bare foot on the rough chunky rock bed. Around midnight, a Baltimore-bound delivery train would come creaking by and then stop at the station in the lower town. It was so long the cars would stretch all the way back with the caboose idling just about where he'd crossed.

Taking a moment to get his bearings, he crept south along the riverbank until he found the patch of familiar ground. A thick screen of scrub trees and tangled brush blocked any view from the Armory or railroad tracks.

"We here," he spoke again gently lowering the sack to the ground. This scabby open area was pocked with a group of faint depressions, reminders of previous visits now nearly obscured by weeds, leaves and foot-high sycamores. The river murmured nearby as it swirled around rocks that looked like patches of bare ground since it had been such a dry summer.

Just beyond the point where the Shenandoah and Potomac merge to become one great river, the mountains—Maryland Heights to the east and Loudoun Heights to the south—meet at the 'gap.' Fishy slowly turned until he had a fix on it. Even with no moon, it was easy to

74

locate since starlight funneled between the rocky slopes down to the Potomac. The gap marked just where the sun rose, heralding the direction home.

As he'd done for all the others, Fishy took up the pick and, sure of his reckoning, stuck the point lightly into the ground then dragged it back two steps to scratch a straight line east-to-west.

The pick bit easily into the sandy soil for a few swings. Then on knees he scooped out the dirt with his gnarly fingers and carefully piled it to the side. When the loose dirt had been removed, he took up the pick again repeating until the hole was about as long as his arm and as deep down as he could reach.

Digging done, he sat on the edge of the hole with his feet in the dark well, the toes of his bare foot pushing loose dirt about in the bottom. He thought back to when he was young and first heard those words of promise, "De spirit moves with de waters, floatin' like a stick 'til he all the way home 'cross de ocean." The respected elder had talked reverently about a distant Homeland. Born not ten miles away, this was all Fishy ever knew about this other 'true' home.

That first time a girl handed him a patched grain sack soft from long use and left without a word, Fishy was already old. From the moment he peered inside, though, somehow he knew what had to be done. Over the years since and always after sundown—a man sometimes, or sometimes a woman—would quietly come to his door. Fishy reached for the sack on his lap brought in the dark earlier this evening. He settled it, folding back the burlap to carefully pull out the newborn. Curled tight with no warmth, it fit in his rough open hand and, even with just starlight, he could see that the skin was pale like the others. Looking at the perfect tiny clenched fingers and toes caused a welling of grief. But he knew why the child had come to rest in his care, because this baby had been fathered by the master.

Fishy slipped the baby under his shirt, the cold lump causing him to suck in a sharp breath.

"Little boy, you's free," he whispered and nodded toward the Potomac. One harsh truth ever burdened him, that from the day of his birth until the day he died he'd never be freed. Cradling the boy more firmly to his breast Fishy wondered, when his own end came, who would free his spirit? Who would carry him to the river?

Handful-by-handful, he carefully dribbled dirt into the hole until it was mounded overfull. With his index finger, he drew an arrow in the soft pile. Quietly rubbing his hands together, he shed the last grains of dirt which fell onto this new wound in the earth. That done, he lay down on top of the tiny mound, the warmth of his skinny belly centered over the loose fill. He would stay there until just before dawn and then get back in time to light the Master's cooking fire.

There was no particular sound he could say alerted him. Yet Fishy's face had just eased on to a comfortable spot when he felt an alarm. There were no large beasts about, he knew; all the deer, bear and cougar had been killed even before he was only a boy. But he felt something, or the presence of someone. It couldn't be the white patrols; they'd have rousted him at gunpoint. His mind scurried. Turning his head slowly to the side, a pair of small bare feet came into view and turning further, he looked up to see a crouching girl easing warily toward him.

Wearing only a baggy shift with her stick arms and legs exposed to the night chill, she squatted beside him. Fishy eased up and without a word of greeting or nod of recognition, sat side-by-side, he cross-legged and she hugging her knees.

"Willie took 'im," she said finally, her head bobbing as her mouth opened against her knee, the words escaping into the night for Fishy to hear.

Willie was her man, but he lived on a farm outside of town with nine other slaves. The young girl lived in Harpers Ferry, alone in a cabin near the top of the hill behind her master's house. Just after dark earlier that evening, the tap had come on Fishy's cabin door. So, the young sinewy man with head bowed must have been Willie, Fishy realized. It was his arm silently extended, trembling so that the sack jiggled in the air as if alive. Fishy knew better.

In all these years, he'd never been followed to this place near the river or been asked what he'd done with the sack. Now here was this girl, and he didn't know what to say. When the low moaning began, his innards knotted because he wasn't sure how to comfort. He'd never had a woman of his own, let alone a child.

"It's alright, Chile', you'll see. All right," he finally cooed. He knew otherwise though; this night's emptiness would never truly heal. Slipping off his jacket, he draped it over the boney shoulders rising and falling as she let out low, sorrowful gasps with each raggedy breath. They sat not speaking, the girl with her head resting on bent knees, arms wrapped tightly around her shins, the old man worrying over how to get this child safely back before Master discovered her gone.

Sitting together in the dark, cackles of laughter and muffled voices occasionally drifted their way from revelers at Fouke's Hotel or the train station.

"Chile', train be comin' soon," he gently prodded, standing up. He hoped to remind her that it was past midnight and if Master or his wife woke needing something, she could be missed.

"Ain't goin' back," she said, working her jaw as if chewing.

The racking spasm following this declaration drew Fishy back to brace himself as if a skittish horse had balked. The girl flopped onto the loose dirt writhing, and beat her fists into the ground. Then just as suddenly, she went limp.

"Ain't goin' back," she slowly repeated.

To see her better, Fishy squatted on his haunches. She sat up, met his eyes and asked, "Where's North?"

"Yonder, 'cross the river," he answered nodding his head, though he wasn't sure how far. Some said a couple of days and others speculated weeks because traveling was only safe at night.

"You ever go there?" she asked, looking out over the flowing water.

"Naw, Chile', never." He slowly shook his head, but it was a lie. She needed to go back and prepare breakfast for her master or they'd both get a whipping or worse.

The girl stood and walked to the riverbank.

More than once Fishy had stood on that shore himself and dreamed of crossing to never return. With the river this low, exposed rocks could almost seem like stepping stones to frog hop to the other side. He knew how deceptive that was. The far shore looked no different than where he was now and the journey from there to freedom was perilous. He knew free blacks and the cabins they lived in were no bigger than his and, doing odd jobs, they still worked for white folk. They had no extra spending money, couldn't buy in white stores even if they did, and there was no schooling for their children. Was it any different up north?

The child had to go back. Fishy went and stood beside her and together they looked across the wide river dappled with reflected starlight.

The girl turned to ask him, "What'd you scratch on Baby's grave?"

Fishy had to think a moment, then answered, "De way down river."

She looked at him, expecting more.

"Baby needs the river to find its way home," he finally said. He had never told anyone about what he did at this place or why. No one had ever asked, but this mother had to know.

The girl turned to stare at the water. He knew she was trying to make up her mind. The other side was a fair distance, but the frequent rocks parting the river made the crossing seem possible. Cautiously, Fishy took her small, calloused hand and waited to see if she'd bolt. After a minute, he gently pulled her away from the water and started inland. In a few steps they stood over the small earthen mound, and he let her hand go. They looked at the dirt disturbed by her earlier grief. Fishy leaned down and dusted away the vestige of his arrow. With his crooked index finger, he scribed a new line. It pointed north.

"Come, Chile'." Fishy straightened with resolution.

Back at the river's edge, he stepped cautiously onto a softly grooved rock that was submerged just beneath the rippling surface. The wisp of a girl followed, her bare feet seeking purchase on the cold indifferent stone, eager to cross.

The end.

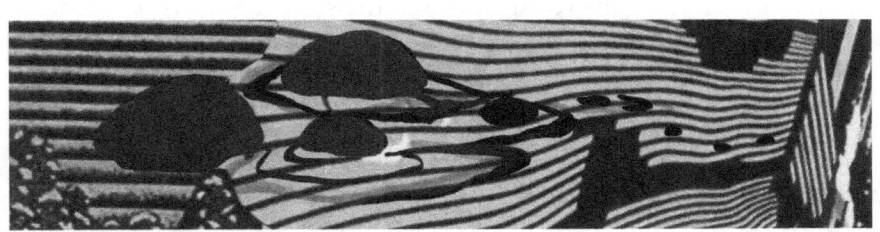

The River Stories
Part Two: Stones in the River

Harpers Ferry, Virginia
Anno Domini 1861

"My name is Mouse. Least, my whole life that's what I've been called. I was born a slave on a farm across the river in Loudoun County, Virginia, and have no memory of my momma or papa . . ."

Without Fishy snoring beside him, Mouse couldn't sleep. His thoughts turned to Old Momma and the stone she'd given him long-ago just before she disappeared. The stone had come from a secret cache she'd kept buried in the corner of the cabin. Every Sunday evening she'd move the iron pot to unearth her 'story' stones then, seated in front of the hearth, Old Momma would whisper to her stones as if gossiping with the ladies after church.

"Why you do that?" young Mouse had finally asked, curiosity over-coming the forbidden sense of her strange, maybe crazy, ritual she guarded so privately.

"They help me remember," she'd said as if this explained it.

"How they do that?" Mouse asked.

Seeming to ignore the question, Old Momma continued sorting her stones before selecting one to her liking. Holding it for a long moment as if breathing into it, she pressed the stone to Mouse's forehead, "This help you remember me."

It was nothing more than any ordinary old river stone, the same he often skipped at the river.

Anticipating his next question, "How it do that?" Old Momma smiled and only said, "You got to talk to it, then it talk back whenever you want."

Now alone and awake with his thoughts, Mouse was remembering. When he was a boy in this very same shack behind Master's house, they'd lived together, him, Old Momma, and Fishy. Until that one morning, when Mouse woke to find Fishy dripping wet and standing head bowed, his arms slack at his sides. Except it wasn't raining yet there he stood trembling in front of the hearth, cold when it should have been warm and crackling from their morning meal Old Momma always cooked.

"You all wet," the boy said, rubbing sleep from his eyes. Then Mouse noticed the big iron pot pushed out of place and the dirt floor dug up where Old Momma kept her buried stones.

"She gone," was all Fishy could say in response to the silent question in the boy's eyes.

"Where she go?"

There'd been no commotion in the night, so Mouse knew Old Momma couldn't have taken sick. But even as a child he'd already heard tales about slaves who, once sold, just disappeared or, if their chance came to run away, left without a word.

Now these many years later, there was no mystery where Fishy had gone. The previous day a deal had been struck with a nearby owner to trade him in exchange for a girl who hadn't yet appeared at the cabin to take his place.

With Fishy absent, Mouse thought back about what Old Momma had said. He remembered the very next day he'd pocketed that stone she'd given him, then down at the river had just skipped it across the water.

"Stones don't never talk," he'd said to himself. "Besides, I can always find me another." After the fourth hop, though, when it sank with a sigh he'd felt inexplicably sad.

Still wakeful, Mouse set his mind to finding another memory stone, that very night. Skirting any house with a dog, he'd made his way down to the Potomac and in the faint starlight, scoured the bank. Plucking a likely candidate from the cold silt, he rubbed the slimy flat stone with his calloused thumb until its dark glistening wetness receded like a raised curtain. Unsure how to get a stone to talk, squeezing it tightly he found Old Momma's words come back to him.

Looking around to make sure he was alone he paused, trying to think of something to say. "I gonna talk to you when I get my own family," Mouse finally whispered. Delaying the question of whether the stone would talk back, he was pleased at the idea that had come to him, to share his innermost hope.

The sky was starting to lighten so he knew it was time he should leave. At a sharp clang, he nearly dropped the rock to run like a rabbit. He realized with relief it was only workers beginning their day at the nearby U.S. Armory. But before his racing heart slowed, he jumped again nearly fit to die as a firm hand clasped his shoulder.

"Steady, boy," the familiar voice cooed, as if calming a bolting horse. "Ain't nobody around 'cept Fishy." The only 'freedom' a slave had was sneaking around at night, but getting caught meant certain punishment.

"Thought you was night patrol," Mouse huffed expelling a long-held breath.

"They thick as fleas since Old Mr. Brown came here to Harpers Ferry and caused such a ruckus," Fishy nodded in understanding, referring to a skirmish at the town armory just a few short weeks ago— planned by a white man, no less.

"Hung him yesterday, so white folk ought to settle down soon," Fishy added. Well, it had been bloody and not a single slave freed, and now the crazy old man was gone to his grave, soon to be forgotten. While feigning disinterest, like every slave in town Mouse had been keenly aware of the goings on. *Could freedom truly ever come?* It was no more than a hint of possibility, and probably just the Devil's temptation the way it had him feeling both exhilarated and scared.

"What you doing out?" Fishy asked quietly. "Looking for a woman?"

"Naw," Mouse said, confused before realizing Fishy was having fun with him. Squeezing the stone tighter, he sure hoped Fishy hadn't seen him talking to it.

"I hear she coming, but I ain't seen her yet," he said.

"You will," Fishy said, adding with a chuckle. "Preacher had to leave go of that girl else his wife going to geld him while he sleeping." The image of Preacher minus his manhood brought a low chuckle from them both. It would be daylight soon but neither seemed ready to leave.

"That be one of them stones?" Fishy said offhandedly.

Nothing got by old Fishy. He meant the ones Old Momma collected even though he hadn't spoken about her all these years, a fact that had never set well with Mouse. Holding out his hand, he unclenched his fist.

"That be a good one," Fishy said casually, as if Mouse was showing him nothing more than a fat root he'd just dug.

"Like one of Old Momma's stones," Mouse almost blurted anger flaring, but kept silent.

Trees and bushes were beginning to take their shape as dawn was giving way to day. If chores weren't done or either man were missed, the alarm would sound to hunt them down. With all the uneasiness caused by Mr. Brown's raid, without a pass from your master it could be dangerous to be caught out.

"Got to ask you something you ain't going to like," Mouse said finally. "Is Old Momma free?"

Fishy bristled. Mouse worried he'd never find out what happened but he'd heard the lore. A few of the older slaves hinted there was a secret spot to cross the Potomac that Fishy knew, and he'd led Old Momma to the other side.

"Why didn't you run, too?" Mouse had always wanted to ask and had imagined Fishy's reply, "'Cause somebody got to watch out for you." But that didn't answer his question about Old Momma's fate.

They stared at each other for a long moment, muscles tensed and nostrils flaring. Clearing this throat, finally Fishy said firmly, "If you ever get a notion to run, best you leave behind any stones before you cross that river."

Without a goodbye, Fishy spun and departed, disappearing into the scrub following a secret path that would take him back up the hill. Mouse turned toward the river and, in fury, flung the stone. *Plip, plip, plip,* and *plop.*

"That all you got to say?" Mouse said, but his anger evaporated as he realized what he'd done.

"No stone ever going to talk to me," he sighed.

*   *   *

As if conjured from thin air, later that day the girl finally appeared. Mouse waved her into the gloom of the shack. He'd heard they call her 'Little'.

"Call me Mouse," was the best he could manage by way of encouragement, his mouth suddenly dry.

Silent, the girl's eyes darted like a starved mongrel ready to bolt. Clutched in one hand she held a small burlap sack with her belongings. The patchwork dress she wore had been pieced together from scraps and twine.

Mouse watched as she tentatively placed one small foot in the hollow of the lower step. After what seemed a lifetime, she finally entered and made a slow circuit of the ten by ten-foot cabin. Her wide eyes took in the furnishings—a straight back chair that Fishy always used, rough plank table they shared for meals, iron cook pots scattered in front of a small fire-blackened hearth and an old shipping crate that Mouse used as a seat. A ladder fashioned from stout tree branches led to a small sleeping loft.

"Gonna be cold tonight," Mouse finally managed, rubbing his hands together, the only thing that happened to come to mind. Little's wary eyes flicked and Mouse could almost hear her thought, *Just like a man wanting to satisfy his needs.*

"I'll fix you a pallet by the hearth," he said quickly. In that moment Mouse somehow felt that this girl, so tiny, light-skinned with tangled wavy hair would change his life. Even knowing slaves weren't allowed to marry, he suddenly ached with yearning, *someday she gonna be my wife.*

"Don't need no help." Little said finally, looking directly at him but as if at some point far beyond.

That night Mouse lay awake in the loft. Little was all that he could think about. A notion came to him that brought a smile, *one day, maybe, he'd have a child with her.*

A faint creak followed by a rustling gave Mouse a start. *What she doin'? She coming up to be my wife?*

"Little?" he whispered to let her know he was awake.

"Go back to sleep, boy, or you'll be waking up in Alabama picking cotton," a gruff voice answered.

When the man had gone, Little climbed up to the loft. Mouse pretended to be asleep but arousal stirred as Little gathered up straw to make a place beside him. Finally she said, "Let's be done with this 'cause all men only want the same thing."

* * *

It would have been a fine Sunday morning except Mouse was confronted by a shadow cast across the doorstep. A massive young Negro man stood waiting outside the cabin, straw hat in hand.

"I come for Little," he said without looking up at Mouse.

"This be Willie," she said and before Mouse could say a thing, Little skirted around him to stand beside the young man twice her size, "He taking me to church."

Every following Sunday sure as daybreak, Willie arrived and solemnly waited outside for Little.

"That boy ain't nothing but an ignorant plough horse that be gone soon as the baby born," Mouse lashed out. The day had come when he could no longer keep denying to himself that Little was showing.

"'Cause Willie such a good worker and I'm a good worker too, his master going to buy me before the baby is born." Her gaze unwavering, Little added, "His master say we can jump the broom." It seemed to Mouse like she was looking directly through him before she turned to leave without another word.

Stunned, Mouse just smoldered, *You ain't going no place!*

* * *

Early on a Sunday morning, Mouse leaned against the far side of a stout oak by the roadside. When Willie came near, Mouse stepped out into the road holding up a hand to waylay him.

"You a damn country boy fool," Mouse began.

"What you mean?" Willie demanded, too surprised to say anything more, giving a dark look to this man he'd always regarded with respect.

"Little gonna have her baby real soon," Mouse said.

Willie stood tall. "Yessir. Master gonna buy her and we jumping the broom!"

"You can jump, but that ain't gonna make that baby yours," Mouse said shaking his head, regarding Willie a long moment.

Quick as a blink, Mouse found himself landed in a tangle of prickly scrub, tossed like he was nothing.

"Preacher been laying with her!" Mouse said, scrambling to his feet. "Master, too, before that horse kicked his head in. If you think your master gonna stay away from her, you a fool. When Little be his property, he do what he want."

Clenching his fists, Willie's eyes narrowed. Mouse held up both hands, not so much to soothe the young man but to point his anger another direction.

"Happens to our women all the time," Mouse said. "When your woman's having a white man's baby, can't nothing be done 'bout it."

Now Willie had an answer. "She say the white men don't mean nothing. My seed is strongest!"

Mouse eyed him with a steady gaze. "Even when the daddy is one of us, you know some babies is white when they born?"

"Course I do," Willie said. But his brow furrowed with uncertainty.

"If the baby one of us, in time he turn to be like you and me," Mouse said indicating Willie, dark as polished walnut or his own skin the color of tanned leather. "Course, it might stay near white. That could be lucky if they ever escape up North where they might pass." He paused to let this sink in. "Trouble is, baby's color don't matter nothin' to the momma."

Willie scrunched his face in distress and confusion.

"'Cause white men been with her, you got to put that baby down," Mouse continued, "just like he the runt of a litter."

"You mean drown it?" Willie said wild-eyed.

"Soon as it's born, while she distracted," Mouse said.

"Then what I do?"

Mouse didn't answer immediately, as if turning over what should be done.

"You put it in a feed sack," he said finally, "wait 'til after dark when all the white people asleep and creep over to Fishy's cabin. He know what to do. Men unable to bear the shame or added burden have done it. 'Only pain and suffering if they stay here,' Fishy say. 'They need to go home.'" Powerless to save the child, yet Fishy could ease its spirit on the journey into the next world.

"Got to do it or forget jumping," Mouse said.

"I already done asked her," Willie said, stricken, "and she give her pledge."

"Yeah but your master be coming around after dark to claim his property," Mouse said. "Ain't nothing you can do about it. He the master. You want people pointing at you the rest of your pitiful life, laughing because you a country boy fool?" Mouse pressed further, "If you a real man, you got to do it."

* * *

Mouse edged warily past the first-floor front parlor. Master lay there in his sick bed, eyes closed, chest barely rising and falling. A vigil lamp burned on a sideboard through the night in case of a miraculous chance he should wake. Above his right eye was an ugly purple hollow the size of a man's fist. Mouse crept to the back stairs his nerves rattling with every creak of a floorboard. He didn't need to worry though, no one else would hear. Still, he stayed quiet even as the Missus, her smell familiar, joined him upstairs in a spare bedroom.

No words passed between them as she nearly smothered him with her fleshy hips and swaying breasts. Missus rocked and moaned, crushing his back and buttocks against the taut ropes suspended on the low post bed barely cushioned by down-filled ticking. When their climax ebbed, and her weight settled on him, Mouse knew she'd soon be asleep.

Drowsy himself, a faint creak brought him alert. At the bedroom door Little stood nostrils flared and chest heaving, rigid as a soldier at attention. She held his eyes as if weighing what to do then disappeared into the darkness. Only after she'd left had Mouse realized the change—her dress was no longer filled out. *By now Willie must have visited Fishy*, he thought, and *Little be mine again real soon.*

Even as the notion warmed him, disquiet settled in his chest. Easing out from beneath the Missus he slipped away thinking he might catch Little. He'd console her, express shock and exclaim doubt that Willie could have ever stolen her baby.

Downstairs, Mouse halted, robbed of breath. There in the sickbed, a pillow partially covered the lifeless face where Master lay twisted but still. The man with such power over them throughout life, in the end had been powerless against a mere sliver of a girl. Mouse swelled with elation, but only for an instant.

"Lord Jesus, girl, what have you done?" he gasped aloud, grimacing as if his gut had been clawed.

Desperate, he frantically straightened the bed covers and tucked the pillow beneath Master's head. As a hasty final gesture, Mouse leaned over and smoothed the man's hair, only in death touching the man who'd owned him all these years. Mouse stood upright, his eyes suddenly leaking tears. Not from sorrow though, but terror, *What will happen to Little and me now?*

Lungs aching, Mouse crashed down the hill hoping to find Fishy at the secret burying place by the river. Fishy would know what to do.

At the bottom of the hill, Mouse pulled up suddenly, nearly tripping over a collapsed dark heap.

"Willie?" Open eyes stared sightlessly at the vast emptiness of the night sky and beneath Willie's head a black puddle gleamed in the moonlight.

"No," Mouse cried out kneeling next to the body, "No! No, no."

Closing the farm boy's eyes, Mouse dragged the body into the thick undergrowth. Snatching up the blood smeared rock, Mouse pushed unsteadily toward the river the best he could, dazed by the mayhem ruling this night. Soon, too soon, town folk would be waking, wondering why their breakfast fires weren't lit. Pistols would be loaded, gear and horses readied and their baying hounds released.

At river's edge, Mouse slung the bloody rock far out into the current. In the still quiet night the only sound was a splash as if a big fish had leaped.

Night chill penetrated his bones as he scoured the banks of the Potomac. A sky full of brilliant stars and a pale moon cast an eerie glow over the river valley, illuminating a scattering of rocks poking above the surface of the wide river.

Mouse had never visited Fishy's secret place. The ghostly light was bright enough for Mouse to recognize tiny depressions as soon as he came across them, scattered, anonymous amongst huddled saplings and a safe distance from the river's edge. The resting place for Little's baby, he knew, would be there. Finally he came across glistening footprints, surely Little's and Fishy's, easy to follow to a fresh mound of grainy dirt that marked the newest tiny grave.

Reality overwhelmed him and tears streamed again. The realization of what he'd done suddenly hit. If he hadn't goaded poor gullible Willie this baby would still be alive. Willie would be alive. Bending closer, he delicately touched the raw scar in the earth where the child had been laid. Then the thought suddenly overwhelmed him, that . . . this child might have been his.

Frantic, Mouse tracked the jumbled footprints to the river's edge. There they seemed to pause for calculation as if gauging the water's mood or the best way to go before plunging ahead. Desperate to escape,

Mouse steeled himself and was just about to step into the pitch-black water when he paused. The shore was littered with stones but reaching down he snatched up one, palm-sized, the shape of a bird's egg and stuffed it in his pocket.

Taking a deep breath he continued, but the slick bottom muck was slippery as ice. Shortening his stride and slowing his pace, he eased away from the familiarity of dry land knowing there was no turning back. Like Old Momma, Fishy and Little, he'd never swum. Once he could no longer touch bottom, he had no idea what would happen. Toeing his way forward, the water rose now and had a distinct pull. The river coursed around nubby rocks and some flat stones but none large enough to be the fabled steppingstones, and no footprints or worn paths to show the way. Clinging to any of these rocks was no refuge; as soon as daylight broke, trackers would spot him immediately.

The next step farther his groin froze as the icy water gripped it, and in that instant his feet lost hold. The current turned him around and pushed him down thrashing and rolling before slamming him against an impassive barrier. He scrabbled up onto the flat surface, wheezing from fear, cold and shock. He rolled over and, breathing heavily, searched the night sky for the North Star, one singular point of hope in the universe.

Mouse roused himself, stood and wiggled his toes to test his balance but, looking down at his feet he realized they could take him no farther. Weariness overtook him and he slumped down on his belly pressing his cheek against the rough surface. Above the whirring river Mouse heard murmuring, like when Old Momma prepared breakfast as he lay in the loft. Hugging the rock offered comfort as he gave in to fear and exhaustion, then he remembered the stone and struggled to retrieve it from his wet pocket.

"How did you cross?" he asked, a tear leaking onto the stone as he recalled the morning Fishy returned soaking wet without her. Just as Old Momma had done when he was a boy, placing the stone against his forehead he said, "Tell me, tell me your story."

'Tween the mountains, Old Man Moon had just cleared the gap so I could see Fishy up ahead. He was hopping from stone to stone like a bullfrog in a hurry. He know'd I was old and my feet no good but he worried about them tracking us. I'd sassed the Missus and knew she meant it this time. She say I be going to auction. When you old and worn out, working the fields picking cotton will kill you quick surely as the sun come up. So I had to leave. Fishy knew a farm where a white family live and they could help me head North. He'd just have to lead me 'cross the river.

"Leave them be!" he'd said. I know I should have listened.

But I couldn't leave my stones behind. Without them I'd have no story, I'd have no past, I'd have no guide on my path. 'Cept the clothes on my back, they all I had. Then that bundle in my sack unbalanced me, and when my stones sank to the deep, I couldn't get free of them.

The eternal river murmured on but the stone fell silent. Now Mouse could hear Fishy's soothing voice, *The river carry the Spirit safely along the start of its journey home* . . . Before that journey, Mouse had one thing left to do. Placing the stone against his lips, in a whisper he began:

"My name is Mouse. Least, my whole life that's what I've been called. I was born a slave on a farm across the river in Loudoun County and have no memory of my momma or papa. When I was a boy, Old Momma and Fishy took care of me like we was family. The farm belonged to the man we called Master . . ."

The end.

The River Stories
Part Three: Carry Me Home

Squinting into the morning sunlight as he stepped off the train at the Harpers Ferry depot, Spencer quickly took in the bustling street scene. Sweaty hard white men unloaded mailbags, crates of produce, and barrels packed with oysters. Store clerks barked at skinny young Negro hands stacking and arranging newly arrived merchandise from Washington, D.C. and Baltimore.

Moving down the platform, Spencer avoided eye contact that would peg him as an uppity Negro, likely one of those troublemakers from the city who didn't know how to behave. Undoubtedly, white men might assume he was a race agitator and some Negroes might think he was a shyster selling burial insurance or hustling patent medicines.

Practiced at being discreet, Spencer occasionally travelled to the South as part of his job. In his head it had seemed simple. He only had to quickly find the old woman: *Miss Little, I'm a researcher with the United States government doing interviews with former slaves. Would you be willing to share your recollections?* Even though he was just an employee from the Federal Writers' Project, he knew race complicated everything.

To make his inquiry, Spencer approached a Negro porter crisp in his blue Pullman uniform, offering his business card. "I'm looking for a Miss Little." *That is,* he thought, *if she's still alive.* The 1930 U.S. Census for Harpers Ferry listed a 'Miss Little' born in 1841 or 1842. The porter's eyes sparked, possibly in recognition, but he said nothing.

"I'm just passing through and would like to hear recollections from someone very old as part of my historical research," Spencer gently pressed.

The porter shook his head. "Best leave the past be." Glancing at the card, he added, "We don't need an outsider stirring up things."

Spencer had a ready reply: "I expect to be gone early tomorrow on the first train to Washington, D.C. and will make sure I'm hardly noticed the short time I'm here."

Shrugging as if to say he had no relevant information, the porter raised his arm and pointed toward High Street. "Try the hotel at the top of the hill. Lots of old-timers up there and it's the only place that rents rooms to us."

After the steep climb uphill from town, Spencer stopped to catch his breath when he reached the sprawling old building. The weathered sign read:

Hilltop Hotel
Rooms to Let by Day or Week
<u>*Colored Gentlemen Only*</u>
No Credit   No Drunks   No Cursing

He felt a tug of reminiscence from half a lifetime ago, back in 1918 when as a young Army corporal he'd marveled at the ruined grandeur of war-ravaged France.

Idlers in the worn, once elegant two-story lobby ignored Spencer, though he was sure every one of them would soon have an opinion on the reason for his visit. Shortly, the whole Negro community would likely be speculating, the Pullman porter would make certain of that. But, Spencer hoped they'd keep it to themselves and leave the white folk out of it.

Upon collecting payment for the night's lodging, the clerk gave Spencer one long look up and down before answering his inquiry.

"Don't know a Miss Little."

Shifting his body so that the idlers couldn't see, Spencer placed two bits on the guest register and turned it back to the clerk, hoping that a quarter would do the trick.

Careful to cover his mouth, the clerk whispered, "There's an old colored man at the stables by the river that will likely talk to you." Then, in a loud voice meant for the idlers, he said, "If you go out for a stroll best leave your hat, tie and bag here so white folk don't think you're one of them trouble makers from the city."

The stable hand's directions to Miss Little's required that he go past the train station to find a path alongside the river. "Folks always watching us," the old man had warned as he insisted Spencer put on a ratty barn coat and tattered straw hat. "Dust up your shoes so they don't shine so much and step lightly."

Nearing the station, Spencer heard the clamor before seeing a group of men on the platform clustered around a message board. They were shouting and gesturing at one another giving Spencer time to duck into a nearby outhouse that had a hand-lettered sign, "Colored."

The stench made him retch even with the door slightly ajar so he could see what the men were up to. Clearly, something had them agitated and Spencer wondered if it might have to do with the recent re-election of FDR or if Germany had invaded another country.

Appearing to reach agreement, the men hurried off with some obvious urgent business to conduct, leaving the platform vacant. Thinking this was his only chance, Spencer lowered his head and shambled to the bulletin board, doing his best to remain inconspicuous.

A telegram message was tacked to the board. Quickly reading the familiar yellow slip, Spencer grasped the urgency:

MARCH 17, 1936 (STOP) HARPERS FERRY, WV (STOP) RECORD FLOOD SURGE OVERFLOWING BANKS ENTIRE LENGTH OF POTOMAC AND SHENANDOAH RIVERS (STOP) RAINS INUNDATE CUMBERLAND AND SHENANDOAH VALLEYS (STOP) TRAIN SERVICE SUSPENDED AS OF 03:00 PM (STOP) LAST TRAIN NOW DEPARTING PITTSBURGH (STOP) MIDNIGHT ARRIVAL HARPERS FERRY (STOP) LAST SERVICE TO WASHINGTON, D.C. UNTIL FURTHER NOTICE (STOP) END MESSAGE (STOP)

Reflexively glancing at the river some thirty feet below the station, Spencer's eyes took in its vast expanse to the far shore and couldn't imagine the amount of water it would take to reach this high to flood the town. *Biblical* is the word that came to mind. Feeling exposed, Spencer hurried and soon located the river path. He vowed to catch the midnight train back to D.C. whether or not he'd interviewed Miss Little.

Troubled by the ominous telegram yet focused on his task, Spencer found Miss Little's cabin not too far upriver even though it was nearly lost amid the tangle of brush, branches, and leaning deadwood. The river was close enough that its soothing gurgle could be heard, prompting Spencer to wonder where Miss Little went if there was high water.

"Miss Little?" Spencer called out.

A sprite of a woman stepped onto the porch and waved him up. After Spencer's introductory spiel, they settled on straight-back chairs. For someone in her nineties she seemed remarkably alert and spry, he thought. Hopefully she had a reliable memory. But first he needed to check if she was aware of the imminent danger headed her way.

"Do you know the river's supposed to flood?"

She sat up a little straighter like a schoolgirl who'd been called on. Smiling she said, "Yes, I've known about the flood all along."

Time being limited, Spencer still wanted to assure himself she'd be okay before asking about slave times. "Is someone coming for you?"

"I expect Fishy be here any time now," she giggled. Her clouded eyes squinted down the path as she kicked her feet out from beneath her long skirt and she leaned forward in her chair.

A grandson, a nephew or some other relative, Spencer assumed. With that settled, he began the formal interview that turned out to be long on generally pleasant memories. It reflected a pattern he'd heard before, a now familiar narrative. "They didn't treat us so bad," and, "Most times we was like family."

Spencer had conducted enough interviews to expect as much but, even so, he approached each interview with expectation. Stubbornly, he just refused to accept the accounts he'd heard consistently, even though he couldn't even pry anything from his own Me Maw. In response to questions, his stubborn grandmother had remained closed-mouth. He'd caught sight of a web of raised markings on her back once while she was sponge bathing. Young at the time, he hadn't realized what they meant. Later, when he'd asked about it, the only thing she'd ever say was, "Nobody wants to hear about them times."

Carefully making his way to the stables, Spencer returned the barn coat and hat before his walk back to the hotel. From a distance he could see a swarm of people as if a hive had been poked. Apparently, word of an impending flood had spurred town folk to begin evacuation. Household furnishings and store merchandise were being piled high on trucks, horse-drawn wagons and handcarts. Stepping lightly as advised, Spencer kept his distance and moved on.

It was getting near full dark when Spencer reached the hotel. Even as he pushed through the gate he could see enough to tell something looked amiss. Perhaps it was just an evening gathering on the veranda, but a group of Negro men clustered in a circle standing over someone slumped in a chair. Fellow lodgers, Spencer thought, perhaps tending to someone ill or discussing the threat of a flood. Then one of them thrust a lantern in his direction. Almost as one, the men turned toward him.

In the light, Spencer caught the accusing look in their eyes. Something bad had happened, that was clear, and likely involved him.

A low moaning escalated to momentary wailing before subsiding as the slumped man pulled at the bloody wrapping around his head.

"This man got beaten 'cause of you," the man holding the lantern said angrily. The hotel clerk let out another loud groan as if to confirm the assertion.

"White folk do this?" Spencer asked evenly. Angry men didn't faze him; he'd dealt with plenty of white soldiers in the Army and crawling across enemy lines on night raids and going bayonet-to-bayonet in trenches with bloodthirsty Huns.

"Stirring things up is what did it," the man said staring intently at Spencer. Then barely containing his fury he added, "White folks want everybody to believe how kindly they was to us. You think they going to let you come along to prove them wrong and not do something 'bout it?"

A familiar figure stepped forward—the train porter, Spencer realized. No longer restraining words of warning, he spoke, "They're drunk, their blood is up and they went looking for you after almost killing this man."

Spencer got the implied message that the clerk held out for as long as he could before sending the vigilantes after him. Surely, they wouldn't harm an old woman if it were he they were after?

The porter interrupted his speculations by adding, "They stole your fancy hat, sliced up your bag and left the neck tie for you," and pointed to a nearby spindly tree where the tie hung limply, fashioned into a crude noose. Underneath, his bag and contents appeared to have been shredded.

"Lucky they got busy clearing out lower town or they'd be hunting you down for sure," another one of them said. "And they going to be looking to bust some of our heads, too, unless the flood drown them."

The porter spoke again, "Before midnight I'll lead you down a back way to the station. Once you're gone maybe they leave us alone."

Nodding his acquiescence seemed to lower the temperature considerably.

After tending to the injured man the group took seats as sentinel to wait out the evening. In the lull, Spencer began to worry over something that occurred to him, "Is anyone besides Fishy looking after Miss Little?"

A ripple of shifting and turning flowed from man to man as if Spencer had said something unseemly. Finally, a match flared and after two puffs the smoker said, "She told you Fishy is coming back?"

"So this Fishy will come look after her?" Spencer said with relief.

"I suppose maybe, if you're one to believe in ghosts," the smoker said. "It's part of her 'prophesy' about the Great Flood that's coming to carry her home across the ocean. She say when it's time, Fishy will return to go with her."

An elder of the group added, "I can't even think how many years ago since he died."

"What?" Spencer nearly blurted. During the long rambling interview that afternoon there had been no mention of any prophesy. Abandoning his assumption that Fishy must be kin and counted on to help her, Spencer also started to question his assessment of Miss Little's mental state.

"She got to be near a hundred years old," one man spoke up.

Alarmed, thoroughly mystified, and worried anew about her safety, Spencer was about to ask if anyone else would look after Miss Little.

"You don't need trouble about her. When she was hardly more than a girl," the smoker said, "she killed her master they say, 'cause he was father of her baby. Then she killed the man who'd pledged to marry her because soon as that baby born he drowned it like a mongrel pup. He wasn't going to raise a white man's child." After a moment he said, "Been hearing that story since I was a boy."

"Will anyone look after her?" Spencer asked in a flurry of muddled confusion and increasing alarm.

"Best let the flood and the Prophesy do their work," one man said. "Just like old Noah, Miss Little gonna go wherever that flood carry her."

A muted growl and an indistinct glow caught their attention. A slow-moving caravan of vehicles strained to make its way up the hill. "They moving to high ground like the rats and other vermin," one of the men said.

The rest of the evening was spent mostly in silent vigil watching the street as a ragged line of cars, trucks, wagons and even handcarts struggled up the long hill going to who knows where. Spencer kept his own counsel but stewed over Miss Little's welfare and the veracity of the stories told about her. What the flood might do to her bothered him more than the possibility that vigilantes had visited, though that was concerning, too. After all, what would they gain harming an old woman?

"Let's go," the porter said, interrupting his thoughts.

Keeping to a back route down to the station, Spencer followed close behind the porter. Within the shadows of the vacant platform, the porter moved over to get a clear view of the river.

"Don't know if the train gonna make it," he said. Bridge lights and a rising moon reflected off the swollen river that now overspread its banks forming a vast, muddy lake. Its center seethed, choked with tangled mounds of branches and whole trees. Then a house, tilted like a sinking ship, slowly drifted by.

While the mesmerizing spectacle distracted the porter, Spencer slipped away. Moonlight helped somewhat, but the encroaching river made it impossible to be sure of the path to Miss Little's. Already ankle deep he knew to keep going against the current that swept past in a thick stew of twigs, branches and leaves. Disoriented and shivering, Spencer wondered if he was crazy, on a fool's errand to rescue Miss Little and perhaps, just maybe, the truth. No. Maybe not crazy. Faint, but unmistakably he heard . . . singing.

A smile spread across his face as he scrambled onto the still dry porch. It wouldn't stay that way for long so he'd have to move quickly, somehow persuade Miss Little to leave her belongings behind then gather her up on his back and carry her to high ground. Not easy but at least possible, he thought with relief, now knowing she was at least safe and unharmed. Not only that, but in high spirits it seemed, having a grand time clapping and singing as if it were a Sunday church gathering:

Wade in the water, wade in the water, children. Wade in the water, God's gonna trouble the water.

"Miss Little?" Spencer yelled, hating to interrupt. Just as he was about to call again, she squealed in delight, "Fishy, that you?"

Fishy? Raising alarm, Spencer thought maybe at least that lent credence to what they'd said at the boarding house.

"Miss Little, it's Spencer. Remember we talked earlier today?"

Without an invitation offered, he pushed the door open and stepped inside. It took a moment for his eyes to adjust to the dark interior. Though indistinct, he found her near the wood stove, sitting cross-legged on a pallet. Yet she didn't greet him with a gesture or rise to meet him. Surely something wasn't right. Had she suffered a spell, was she confused?

"It's Spencer," he said in his softest voice. Water gurgled up between floorboards as he inched forward.

"Fishy?" Miss Little said, lifting her head.

Squinting in the darkness, Spencer first made out his fedora, too big for her head slanted down over her eyes. A slight glint drew his attention to her wrists and then her neck. It was like a re-creation of an old tintype he'd seen once, of a slave draped in chains. But here they also wound around the cast-iron cookstove so that, what, to be sure an old woman could make no escape? Or, could it be, to make sure he made no escape?

"I . . . I've . . . come back," he croaked, struggling to find his voice.

Gently raising the fedora, he gasped. Only patchy stubble remained where her abundant silver mane had been hacked off. Furiously tossing away the hat, Spencer failed to notice her glow of grace, of the smile on Miss Little's face.

"Fishy, sit down," she beckoned, patting the straw covered pallet next to her like old friends that needed to catch up. "I've been waiting the longest time for you to come back."

Worse than despair he'd felt in the cold muddy trenches of France, Spencer shook his head and lowered himself to the floor. Full realization hit that he was the one who had brought this upon Miss Little.

Taking his hand, she said, "Fishy, I got things to tell you before God stir the waters that will carry us home." Spencer lightly squeezed her hand, encouraging her to begin.

"Remember that night before we escaped across the river?" she began with a smile of long-ago recollection. "I'd hid behind some bushes and watched you bury my new baby. Then when I showed myself, I scairt you nearly half to death.

"You told me to hurry back up the hill, 'Master be looking for you soon,' you said. Then I tell you, 'Ain't goin' back.' But you didn't know why, and all these years I never did tell. Did you suspect? You didn't know that I had to run. I had no choice. I'd just killed two men."

"Oh!" Spencer drew in a sharp breath. The bits of information began to fit. It wasn't just hearsay the men had been relating. Had there even been a touch of pride in Miss Little? Yet what of the danger, possibly to every one of them, if her story fell on the wrong ears? Could it be, though, that maybe they wanted the world to learn of it someday so they'd said enough to make sure Spencer got it right?

"Remind me what happened next?" Spencer coaxed, grasping for something to focus on other than the endgame that was rapidly approaching with the rising water.

"You know Willie and me was gonna jump the broom? But just as my baby was about to be born, he took to drinking and actin' like a crazy man. 'I ain't raising no white man's child,' he'd rant, convinced Master Tom was the father, not him. When other men had been shamed, Willie knew they brought babies to you. That's why he came to you to bury my baby. I never dared ask, did you know it was Willie killed my little boy?"

After a moment of quiet, Miss Little continued, "But this is the part you never knew . . ."

Straw bedding dislodged and slowly began swirling around them along with kindling, a bowl and wooden spoon. Spencer had read about the land of the Nile where the Pharaohs ordered all their worldly goods to be buried alongside them when they died to prepare for their comfort in the next world. The thought came unbidden and offered no comfort at all.

"That baby was my own flesh and blood," Miss Little said. "When I woke and knew what Willie done, I swear right then, *an eye for a eye*."

"Master Tom had been laying in that sick room for ever so long never waking after he got kicked in the head by that horse. You recall that, Fishy? Before that trouble, though, he was free enough about laying with me. Even with the Missus asleep upstairs, I went to Master Tom's sickbed that night and made sure he'd never trouble any young girl again. I took the pillow from under his head and smothered him to death."

Spencer listened grimly.

"Then I went searching for Willie. I found him coming back up the path from the river. He got down on his knees blubbering, begging and crying for forgiveness. But just like he were a snake, I snatched up a rock and strike him dead."

The chains rattled as she slammed her small hands down splashing both of them. Slowly her smile returned, seemingly satisfied she'd made her point.

"Fishy, how you got me talking sideways. I've got to be sure and tell you about the Prophesy."

Water now up over his legs, Spencer knew soon he'd start bobbing alongside Miss Little. It reminded him of crouching beside a doomed comrade offering meager comfort all the while wondering how he'd act in his own final moments.

"Go on, tell me," he said, steeling resolve as he had a lifetime ago in the impending doom crawling across no man's land.

"After the War when we come back here," Miss Little continued, "you recollect that hellfire preacher and his brood of ladies that come to Christianize me? When Preacher dunked me in the river, instead of Jesus, a Prophesy came to me. It say that when the river has a mind to, it will carry us all home."

Smiling she said, "Fishy, they're calling. Can you hear?"

I'm going to see my momma, I'm going to see my papa, I'm going to see my baby, when the river carry us home. Feel that river rising, feel their spirits rise; to the far, far shore, to the far away shore, we're going home.

Spencer could hear no calling, could see no Prophesy, but the water's furious rise forced him to decide.

As Miss Little's hand slipped from his, Spencer whispered, "Godspeed," on her voyage home as he began his own journey to carry her story throughout the land.

The end.

Author's Note: While this story is fiction, there was an effort to collect oral histories from former slaves by the Federal Writers' Project from 1936 to 1938. More than 2,300 first-person accounts were collected in what came to be known as the Slave Narrative Project. The collection is available on-line from the Library of Congress by searching for: "Born in Slavery: Slave Narratives from the Federal Writers'

Project, 1936 to 1938."

And,

On March 18-19, 1936, Harpers Ferry, West Virginia was inundated with floodwaters that were the highest ever recorded at 36.5 feet. Many businesses and houses in Lower Town were destroyed or left in ruins and bridges across the Potomac and Shenandoah Rivers were swept away.

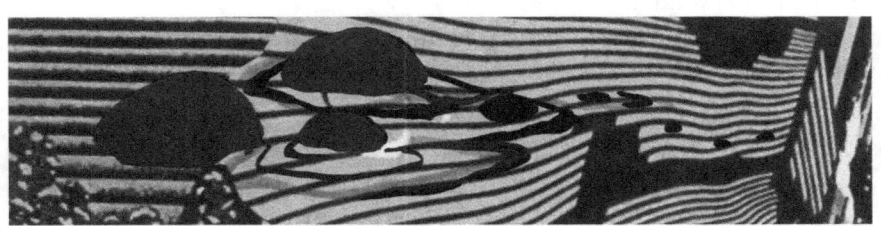

Pleasant Dreams, Google

Chief leads the way down the rickety wooden stairs to the basement of the old courthouse and shoves open the rusted metal door to impenetrable blackness. The air is still as death.

While Chief feels blindly for a light switch, I want to say, "A black hole is a region of spacetime from which nothing, not even light, can escape." I bite my lip or else would continue, "An event horizon surrounds a black hole and marks the point of no return."

Mum is the word, though. But I'll keep a weather eye open and my guard up until the day's events, or lack of them, proves I can relax. I wish I hadn't thought about the point of no return.

Every summer my high school counselor has gotten me a job with the county as a maintenance helper. "This time," he told me firmly, "Keep your mouth shut, head down, do what they tell you and at summer's end you might get on fulltime." He gave me this advice because I know lots of different things and can talk a blue streak, which sometimes gets me into trouble. That's how I got my nickname, Google.

Finally, Chief finds a dangling string and yanks it, turning on a tiny naked light bulb. I feel a little better but not having my phone leaves me anxious,

101

disconnected from the real world. "You're here to work and not play on your goddamn phone," the Chief said before we'd left the shop. It's resting on the shelf in my locker next to the paper bag with my lunch—a baloney sandwich and an apple—instead of in my back pocket.

As my eyes adjust to the weak light in the basement, Chief says, "Maybe, you can't screw up this time," and with tattooed arms folded over his barrel chest he nods toward what might be an event horizon. A black hole could be lurking just beyond it.

A jumble of broken furniture, old office machines, wobbly-looking stacks of cardboard boxes and multitudes of other potentially unstable things define the outer edge where absolute blackness begins.

"All this crap needs to get tossed while court is closed for renovation. Anything you can carry goes out to the dumpster. Leave the heavy shit for someone else." Chief waits because he knows from past summers that I have a talent for being a motor mouth.

Keeping my lips zipped is nearly impossible. I'd almost spilled the beans on our descent to this netherworld beneath the courthouse. Each step downward reminded me of portals to the underworld, Lascaux cave paintings, root cellars, storm cellars, wine cellars, dungeons with and without dragons, Mother Earth, Mr. Badger and Mole, Hobbits, Speleology or the likelihood of spotting a gate sporting a Latin inscription telling me emphatically to abandon all hope. Even Freud considered the subconscious a creepy storage space beneath the conscious mind, only to be probed with trepidation because it is dark and scary as Hell like this basement.

Mouse-quiet, I vigorously nod my reply thereby conveying that I understand my job is to remove crap, slang for feces, and leave behind heavy fecal matter. I think of the dead and how once every muscle in the body lets go they inevitably shit. Obviously, the Chief does not comprehend the extent of what could be lurking in the below-grade world or the far dark corners of the mind. Both can be dangerous if probed by the unwitting.

A single word from me could alert Chief but my operational imperatives are simple: head down, yap shut and throw-out shit. I really need a fulltime job because at summer's end my parents are retiring to Florida and made it clear I won't be going with them.

Chief says, "You got two weeks, understand?"

I want to say, "That's 14 days, 336 hours, 20,160 minutes, or 1,209,600 seconds." But I just nod again like a bobble doll on a dashboard without looking directly at him, thereby signaling silently that I comprehend the length of time allotted for disposal of crap cluttering this dark, subterranean cavity that may be a metaphor for many things real and imagined.

Chief turns to go and, staring at the space where he'd just stood, I think of a vacuum that is a state of emptiness, a void, like when Mom and Dad retire to Florida or like a day long ago when my little brother sank into an event horizon never to return. Nearby in a sandbox, I was making foxholes for tiny plastic soldiers and just through a scraggly hedge my parents dallied over cocktails with neighbors. I'd like to believe that that sad Sunday afternoon had already been scripted as a few scribbled lines in the Divine Plan. If true, it was God's will and I'm off the hook. But, that kind of knowledge is hard to come by and may never be revealed to me.

Chief lifts his work-booted foot onto the first stair step to ascend to the bright outer world and then freezes. To respond or not seems to be on his mind as I land on his broad back like an irritating gnat with all the moxie a ninety-eight pound weakling can muster.

"You idiot!" he finally growls, while slapping and dancing a jig to dislodge me.

I sometimes act in socially inappropriate, though usually harmless, ways. Even to me, this impulsive leap had overtones of mental instability. Luckily, playing horsey with Chief lasted exactly one second which is 1/60th of a minute, 1/3,600th of an hour or 1/86,400th of a day. My bizarre behavior might be excused if Chief thought I was indulging in horse play that regular guys and average Joes do for a laugh while at work.

It's done to make time go faster, re-enforcing Einstein's notion that time is elastic and results in more screwing-off at work rather than less. Thank you, Albert.

I had those thoughts in the nanosecond it took for him to shake me off onto the dirt floor—right after I bit his ear.

From my new vantage point, time seemingly stops as Chief scrunches his now red face into crinkles resembling a vine ripe tomato, the official fruit of Ohio, the Buckeye State.

"Christ, now what?" Chief grunts angrily, though his non-verbal communication expresses a modicum of parental concern. Wincing, he rubs his injured ear.

Taking inventory of myself to ascertain the cause of his apparent anxiety leaves me clueless. True, I'd landed on the cold ground and was now blubbering uncontrollably but not because he'd flicked me like a flea off his back. All I did was try to hitch a ride out of Hades waiting room and only bit him because I was afraid to be left behind. Now, I might get fired because biting a supervisor is probably not allowed, even for a good reason like not wanting to be sucked into a black hole.

Yanking me roughly to my feet and giving me a shake, Chief shouts,

"Get a hold of yourself."

He seems ready to box my ears if I don't quickly turn off the faucets. I want to tell him that my weeping and gnashing of teeth is from fear of the darkness, but maintain radio silence still hopeful I'll be forgiven.

"Are you claustrophobic?" he asks and relaxes his grip on my spindly arm, which I take to mean he isn't sure of his clinical diagnosis. Standing in this space, possibly on the precipice, he could have guessed Thanatophobia, from Thanatos, the Greek personification of death, the non-state when the chalk marks for our good and bad deeds are finally tallied while we nervously await the results before Him, Her or It—whatever the Uber Deity is.

Still, the cat keeps my tongue while my head bobbles another "yes." Clearly, he doesn't realize that we might be standing in front of a one-way portal to deep, dark space or, if implausibly lucky, only a few steps from a wall decorated with charcoal drawings of grazing bison, cavorting horses and majestic elk last seen 30,000 years ago by the flickering light of a smoky torch. Yet, Chief acts as if this place could only be a damp, cluttered basement under an old brick courthouse long overdue for a thorough cleaning.

Wiping my eyes, I wonder if there were old paper files of death records down here in dead storage, a fitting place to keep such things.

"Christ," he says disgustedly and symbolically washes his hands of me with a shove, probably because there isn't any germicidal soap handy.

Christ, I think, is nowhere around.

To stop any more pushing, I hold up my hands. They are blackened and corrupt because I haven't washed them in a very long time. At least my river of tears has slowed to a trickle and this is probably Chief's chief concern. Still, I keep my head down not allowing him even a peek through the smudged windows of my dark soul. I can only hope that a good angel will alight on his muscular shoulder and whisper my case so I can keep my job and save enough money to go to community college next year.

After a contemplative pause to gather his thoughts, Chief says, "Let's find some water and get you cleaned up."

Undoubtedly, this is a sincere gesture meant to convey that, as a fatherly type, he understands that young men sometimes hit rough patches and should be helped whether or not they want or need it. What he can't know is that water, $H2O$, one of the four classical elements, a cleanser for both body and soul, covering 70.9 percent of the earth's surface, the source of all life and the wellspring of the River Styx, is the font of my phobias, the warm welcoming water that filled our benign backyard wading pool so many years ago, and is the source of all my woes.

Slapping his hands together he says, "Let's go."

I sense his sympathetic, but firm paw reaching for me. A rabbit wearing a top hat and holding a pocket watch doesn't need to show me the way. I dart for the demarcation line of jumbled furniture and wobbly boxes, crossing my fingers, hoping while hopping, that an event horizon is not in my immediate future.

"What the . . .?" Chief calls out as I retreat into the heart of darkness.

Wiggling and worming into the unknown, I have no direction or destination. Bellying like a blind snake, I slither until I can go no further. Eventually, I hit what has to be the cool, smooth surface of a foundation wall and stop dead in my meager tracks.

Once my breathing returns to a resting rate of fifteen breaths per minute and my heart rate slows to a respectable seventy beats per minute, I can hear the exasperated Chief sighing, "Google, get out here now or I'll come in and get you." This is followed by repeated shouts, "Google," a three-beat pause, "Google," gradually shifting from boss angry to increasing paternal concern for a child who's strayed.

Soon I hear crap being tossed about and know my goose is cooked even though my temperature has not reached 165 degrees as recommended by the USDA for a whole, young bird. Is it high time to step out of time as Heidegger suggested, let go of time's linear arrow and drop like a rock into the abyss or simply shimmy off a curb into oncoming traffic?

It takes me one sliver of time, another nanosecond, to screw up my courage and decide on a long shot, to script my own ending even if in the end Chief rewrites it. Chief's part will be played by Chief moving toward me through the darkness as fast as an asteroid on target for a disastrous collision with Mother Earth.

Side note: I know Chief could not physically move at 186,282 miles per hour, but this simile alerts the reader that things will move quickly and not well for me.

Back to my script idea: nail-biting readers will be wondering if I'll have enough time to scribble a happy ending before Chief douses me with a pail of soapy water and starts rub, dub, dubbing me to death with a spanking new Fuller brush.

Working Title: Pleasant Dreams

Some 25,000 years have elapsed since the last human-like species, Neanderthal, died out, leaving Homo sapiens in dominion over the earth until the moment of my slinking return into the primordial darkness from whence the first simple animals timidly crept out of the muck a half billion years ago.

This sets the stage for a stage without lights, a lonely but imaginative waif sans friends who hopes for the slimmest hope of escape, if it can be sprung from the eternal. To counter this tiny bit of optimism is the hard-nosed but well-meaning Chief, cast as the villain, playing the part of a biblical bully under the persuasive thumb of the Almighty, inspired to enforce the passage: Cleanse your hands, you sinners (James 4:8), even for those whose hands cannot be cleansed with soap alone.

Before Chief roots me out and Spic and Spans the daylights out of me or I miraculously escape by heaving a so-called Hail Mary pass with a second remaining on my clock, I have one thing to do that is at the heart of this drama. The prop I need is an unassuming lump of sky-blue chalk that has been slumbering in my pocket for years quietly waiting a turn at stardom.

On the smooth wall in front of me, I begin blindly drawing a face as best as I can remember. How it turns out won't matter because it's dark as coal tar in this hidey-hole. Taking a half step backward, I squint to see my progress even though I can't see the end of my nose. Perhaps it's a trick of the light or lack thereof, or the fact that the big bad wolf is pounding on the door, but I can actually see the cherubic face of my baby brother from long, long ago.

Satisfied with mission nearly accomplished, I step up and inscribe my work:

I'm sorry,
Love, Google

Now that I've almost reached what should be the grand finale, the symbolic lowering of the curtain, I have a sudden flash of inspiration or perhaps desperation as I remember the theoretical possibility of time travel to a parallel universe. Truly, this is the longest of long shots, the floppy-eared rabbit that gets pulled out of a top hat and scoring the winning mega millions lottery ticket all rolled into one. Is it possible that this pit of darkness that is dense with moldy things from the past, laden with my present dire situation and overshadowed by what may be my dubious future, may actually be the mythical Kerr's Black Hole where time travel is theoretically possible? If so, I might find a way to slip into one of many parallel universes as if this whole shebang is one big loaf of bread while we blithely live in just a single slice. Then, I could simply gnaw my way into a different past, present and future like a hungry mouse.

"Google!" Chief shouts and I know that only the thinnest of membranes or piles of crap separate me from my impending fate.

Deciding that cleaning my own slate is preferable to having my slate wiped clean by Chief, I beat a hasty retreat. Burrowing deeper and deeper into the unknown, I finally come upon a scraggly hedge and just beyond it my parents are laughing over cocktails with neighbors in the warm afternoon sunshine. Leaving my tin of soldiers in the sandbox, I pick up the garden hose and begin filling the wading pool. As it rises, my little brother giggles and slaps at the water. When the pool is half full, I turn off the spigot and join him until mother shouts, "Time for dinner!" It's Sunday and we'll be having roast pork and sauerkraut, my favorite.

Pleasant dreams, Google.

The end.

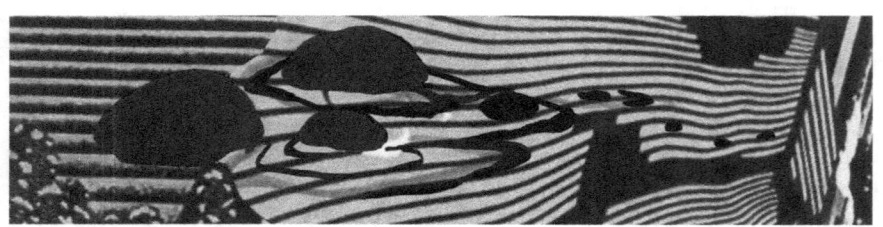

Get Moving

Home from work, Beth flopped on the old sofa while Hemingway pawed the front door wanting to go outside. With eyes half-closed, she watched the dog and wished never to move again.

There was a clawed-out hollow in the lower door panel from the dog's adamant signal for his evening walk. Age had reduced his bark to a throaty grunt. In dog years, Hemingway should have retired and moved to Florida ages ago.

"Come here, Baby," Beth urged, patting the sofa, hoping without an ounce of optimism that just this once he'd skip their evening routine. They'd been together longer than her marriage. The persistent scratching and grunting continued.

"All right, all right . . ." Beth resigned to her fate. Hemingway's rear end went into a frenzy of wiggles and wagging. Moving her own legs and arms though felt like lifting burlap sacks of wet sand. Their evening walk was now her only exercise.

They used to jog. Her legs and lungs enjoyed the challenge of their nightly romp through the neighborhood to the park and back. Then muscle and joint pain took longer and longer to heal until she ached most of the time. Hemingway matched her physical travails with his own degenerative hip that required daily medication.

"I guess we're both getting old," she had consoled him, as their route shortened to hanging around the front yard until he did his business. Then her husband moved out, and nightly walks, regardless of pain, helped fill up the evenings better than sitcoms.

Hemingway came over and nudged Beth just below the knee with his cold wet nose. After giving her a hopeful look, he trotted back to the door, his nails clicking on the oak floor.

Once they were outdoors he transformed, straining at the leash like an eager puppy. He huffed loudly, only stopping to sniff then mark his territory. Pulled along, Beth's brain mechanically inventoried her aches, sounding an alarm when something was worse or new. Her shoulder seemed to take the strain okay, but her kneecap felt like it wanted to pop loose whenever she started down an incline.

There was the deeper sense of drag, too.

Soon they would both have to face the move to someplace new and she didn't want to even think about packing. The divorce settlement stipulated that the house be sold and the equity divided. Each Sunday she meant to search the classifieds for another house to rent and bought a fat newspaper. A wobbly stack was ready for recycling and she hadn't called one real estate agent.

She'd need someplace just big enough for her books and her dog. There were lots of books, mostly second hand. Her husband sneezed violently when he got near them. Dog dander aggravated his psoriasis, and something endemic to the house, probably mold or mites, made him wheeze. Come to think of it, he was probably allergic to her too.

"I feel better as soon as I leave this house," he'd claimed, often enough. Lately, he must be feeling pretty darn good.

Hemingway lunged at something rustling in a pile of leaves, jerking the leash sending a jolt of pain through her shoulder. It was less than the other one she felt.

She, on the other hand, had loved the house ever since they found it. It meant they had finally grown up, getting settled after years of graduate schools and tiny apartments. She had filled the rooms with secondhand furniture. The sunny, south-facing room was going to be the nursery. The room gradually became the study after years of trying gave way to little then no hope that she'd ever get pregnant.

He could use some of the furniture, he claimed, if it could be doused with disinfectant. Whatever; she didn't care. For twelve years she'd lived with him and his growing distance from her, and any lingering sympathetic feelings were exhausted.

Hemingway had always been hers. On this evening, he pulled her along as usual in front of glowing houses that emitted the mingled sounds of TV newscasts, golden oldies, and children yelling at one another. He knew exactly the point where they always turned off into a heavily wooded park. It had a neglected blacktop path laced with cracks filled with grass. When they finally entered the park, there was still enough daylight left to penetrate the tree canopy and keep evil spirits and teenage hoodlums at bay.

Walking deeper and deeper into the park, she eventually reached a place that gave her ironic comfort because it was vaguely domesticated. There was a washing machine with the lid yawning open waiting for a load of dirty clothes. A single high-top tennis shoe lay nearby and seemed in some way related. Serenely at home in the mud of a nearly dry creek bed stood an upright tarnished brass floor lamp with a canary yellow shade. Lichen-covered rocks mingled easily with lichen-covered tires. Beth never participated in the annual park clean-up day. The trash didn't bother her that much.

Hemingway slackened his pace considerably as they walked up the long stretch of blacktop, heading back toward the street. Soon, he was huffing, the leash slack. The park was creepy in full dark and Beth scratched the dog's ear and quietly coaxed, "Come on, Baby, you can make it."

The dog parked himself suddenly, tongue lolling and wiggling limply from his mouth. Streetlights came on in the distance as the darkness slowly moved in.

Beth was grateful for the rest, though anxious to get out of the park. Her left knee was throbbing. Watching Hemingway for signs of recovery, her attention was caught by some fresh painting on the blacktop a short distance ahead of them. Moving as far as the leash allowed, she read:

GET

HIGH

DRUNK

LAID

The words were spray-painted in squiggly silver script. It had to be a guy. At first, she imagined a skinny street-wise fifteen-year old. He'd be spraying with one hand while his other clutched the waist of his baggy pants so his butt wouldn't show completely. Except these days it could just as easily have been some smart-mouth nine-year old.

A gentle pull on the leash told Beth it was time to go. She glanced distractedly at Hemingway and then returned her gaze to the words. Their brash directness poked at her insides. For just a second, all her moribund longings swarmed like bees.

There had been much younger days, and quiet dark evenings in parks like this one. There had been long nights when she had wanted her husband. And he had wanted her.

The bees slowly vanished, their buzzing faded into the night.

She strained to listen for their return; all that came back was the sound of her husband driving away the last time she saw him. She stood there, trying to remember. Something from so long ago.

Hemingway had heaved himself up from the blacktop and lost patience. With a tug on the leash, he yanked Beth into motion.

"Get," she whispered, stepping over the word *get*, but couldn't formulate her own silvery blacktop proclamation. Trailing along behind Hemingway she kept repeating, "Get, get, get . . . " without getting anywhere. When they exited the park, the leash went slack and the dog gave a slobbery shake of his jowls. They'd been gone thirty-five minutes and Hemingway was now almost out of gas.

"You're an old puppy," she crooned softly, pressing the dog against her chest, gently stroking his head. "Yes, you are."

He trailed Beth for several slow blocks. She was careful not to pull on the leash.

"Okay, Baby," she said, and knowing that her body was going to protest, she picked him up. Cradling Hemingway like an infant, she carried him the last remaining blocks to home. Pain sawed into her shoulder and her knee felt swollen, so hot she half expected it to glow in the dark. Once on the front porch, she sat down stiffly in the cold metal chair, feeling the rust pits through her clothes on her back and bottom. The dog's eyes were glazed and he panted loudly.

A car passed slowly, as if searching for a house number. She thought for a moment they might stop and yell if she knew where so-and-so lived. Twelve years and she only knew the neighbors on either side of her house. They had whole histories they shared freely with her, shouting across their porches or catching her at the curb when she was putting out the trash. They'd proudly announced the arrival of a new grandchild or offered to show their stitches from triple bypass surgery. She'd listened attentively and answered, "That's wonderful," or "Is that right?" and offered nothing about herself.

Get, get, get . . .

For some reason, she was reminded of her junior year at Ohio State moving into her first apartment with four girlfriends. Energy had crackled in the air as they raced to early morning classes on Renaissance art, had late night conversations that really mattered, drank endless cups of coffee, and madly loved pale boys who quoted Ginsburg and Dylan and whispered in the dark, "I'll be careful, I promise."

She gently stroked Hemingway's coat and felt his heart beating through her sweatshirt. The air was growing chilly and she winced at the thought of standing up. At the moment it seemed impossible that Beatlemania, ending war, and reading Jane Austen had been—still were?—her treasured passions.

Now all she wanted was to . . . get by. There it was, as if she'd just sprayed the words on the porch floor.

GET
BY

Get coffee would be nice too. Get Starbucks, even better. That would be a comfort. But she'd have to get up to do that and she didn't want to get moving just yet.

Hemingway had collapsed against her chest, snoring, and now jerked in his sleep, as if in his dream he were chasing the thing rustling in the leaves that he had long ago lost the energy to catch.

"It's okay, Baby," she said to herself as much as to the dog. In the dark, she rocked the chair, enjoyed Hemingway's warmth, and slipped backwards in time.

In graduate school she'd met Mr. Right: tall, bright, athletic and except for thick black glasses, a real hunk. English lit was her major and he was studying architecture. How quickly in succession time had pressed her to get real, get married, get settled, get established, get pregnant, get hired, get promoted, get tenure, get it. The wedding toasts never mentioned the part about get depressed, get fired, get therapy, get better, get worse, get wise, get stuck, get older, get hurt, get divorced, get out.

She thought briefly about saying or doing something that might get her husband to come back. Was that it? Having him back? Anything, however empty, to fill the evenings.

Get, get, get. How had she gotten stuck with a romance novelist penning her early years and a soap opera writer scribing a hackneyed mess of the last few chapters? If only a Fairy Godmother could wave her magic wand and revise the whole script. There wouldn't be so many scenes where she had to *get* something.

To hell with *get*.

The heroine could just *be*: be wise, be happy, be loved, and be done.

By now Beth's sleeve was soaked with drool as she murmured comforts into Hemingway's floppy ear.

He sighed loudly and twitched every so often.

She sighed too and clutched him tighter.

"We'll move to a new house," she cooed. "And there'll be a big park nearby for us to play in."

The dog calmed, his breathing quieted, and his eyes closed.

"If we don't," she said softly, resting her chin on his bony head, "it'll all be okay."

The end.

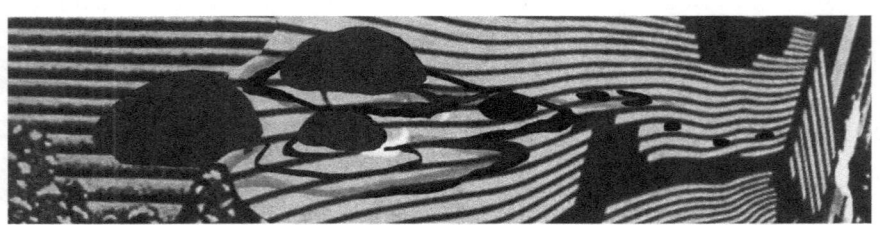

Drivers Education

Sunday morning, and I drove. My fifteen-year-old Samantha, formerly Sammy, was in the car with me acting her usual sullen self. "Samantha" was what she wanted to be called nowadays, but I kept slipping up earning me additional dirty looks and her stock rebuke, "I'm not a child anymore."

It was time for her first driving lesson but practicing on the busy streets of our slice of suburbia would make me a nervous wreck. I needed to find some place not so crowded. Walmart had a huge parking lot. The traffic light changed. We rolled up beside one of those roadside milk crate shrines with a scrap wood cross that was twined with plastic roses. A raggedy stuffed bear clutched the string of a balloon that gently swayed in the wind. It read, "Daddy we'll miss U 4 ever!"

Will she? I had my doubts.

Lately, Samantha hid in her room or was out with friends. Her new mantra was, "I can't wait to go to college in California." Paying for that and all the other bills will keep me working until I drop dead.

Undoubtedly the silvery balloon swaying above my headstone will read, "Daddy we'll miss your credit card 4 ever!"

Samantha speared the radio tuning button with the chipped neon nail of her index finger. Loud thumping music was punishment for not letting her bring her IPod or whatever those things are called. I can't keep them straight. The list of things I didn't like was growing by the day—always on her cellphone, the garish lipstick and eye shadow, tee shirts stretched way too tight, shorts too short, smart mouth, and hiding in her room texting friends, going on Facebook or doing whatever teenagers did alone nowadays. Her mother didn't seem to mind, "She's just being a normal teenager."

"Turn it down," I grumped, the music scrambling my brain waves. Talk about a dumb idea. I'd hoped that these driving lessons might help retrieve some of the feeling of the days when she was Sammy and save a few bucks, to boot.

Samantha lazily poked the volume but the music seemed louder. Her head bobbed and her hands drummed the dashboard.

"Enough!" I yelled, jabbing the power button. The light changed and I pressed on the gas. I joined the line of cars snaking into Walmart but quickly bailed out. There must have been five hundred on the lot already.

"Save. And be saved," I joked, trying to lighten things a bit. "If Walmart was a mega church, they'd save mega souls too!"

Ignoring me, she slouched against the seat tightly hugging herself.

No good. I needed a new road map to guide me. She'd say get a GPS. That and Twitter and a thousand other things were her world and me just a confused visitor from the last century and another planet.

Not sure where to try next, I was grateful the light at the bypass skipped to red and gave me time to think and explain myself. "It . . . " I hesitated for a moment unsure what I could say without getting into a fight. "I don't like that kind of music."

"You only like stuff from the dark ages," she spat back.

I wanted to say, "Like when this town only had three traffic lights?" That seemed like a hundred years ago, before families wanting a better life and willing to make the long commute into Washington, D.C. moved here. Now, the high school had more students than the entire town population when I was growing up. Acres of spanking new houses covered the old fields where we used to hunt for arrowheads after spring plowing. We'd get a nickel for ones that weren't broken and spend the money on Cokes and stick pretzels. More proof that I was a useless relic from another time.

Not wanting to give her more ammo, I kept quiet and hit the power button filling the car with headache inducing music. Tapping madly on the steering wheel as if keeping time, I'd surely earn a sideways grimace from her. Tough. One more embarrassment wouldn't make any damn difference.

As the light turned green, I thought of a place for driving practice. Afterwards I'd treat her to an ice cream soda at that retro diner that was supposed to be a popular new teen hangout.

Samantha fidgeted, thinking, or perhaps just as likely off in her own world. I was reminded of when she was a baby and I carried her. She'd always squirmed and kicked, impatient to get down and be on her own. At the time, it seemed so far off but even now it was hard to imagine.

"Jesus!" I yelped, jerking the wheel to the left.

A blurry haze had leapt from the curb. Or had it? Probably just some leaves blowing around. Samantha's hands shot out at the same moment, palms bracing flat against the dash.

"What?" she squealed, her high excited pitch indicating she was scared but not sure why. The indistinct *thump-thump* could have been anything, probably only the toolbox banging around in the trunk.

"Nothing," I answered quickly.

"Daddy," Samantha managed to say, "was that an animal?" She whipped her head around to look out the rear window.

"What if it was someone's pet?" she pleaded, spinning back to face me. Her usual scrubbed pink face had blanched to ghostly white. In contrast, the carefully applied red lip-gloss made her mouth seem clownish though her eyes said she was deadly serious.

"No Sammy, it wasn't." I answered loudly, knowing I wasn't about to go back and find somebody else's kid crying and hating me too.

I drove on and music filled the car again. "Just the spare sliding around in the trunk, Samantha," I said, though without much conviction.

She turned off the radio. "Animals have rights, too, and you can't just run over them."

I knew better than to argue and in silence we drove to an upscale housing development under construction west of town, one of many that seemed to sprout up like mushrooms after a spring shower. But it would be perfect for the first lesson of Drivers Education. Compacted gravel roads crisscrossed acres of bare, roughly graded building lots.

One model home and a few skeletal house frames perched on cinder block foundations gave a ghostly hint of what was to come.

Oddly enough, this lonely place gave me the tiniest bit of optimism, though my hands were still sweaty. It seemed whenever I was around her lately I was primed to be angry about something—her weird outfits, too much makeup or her smug know-it-all attitude.

"Here we go, girl!" I said, brightly reminding myself to keep my cool no matter what. Reaching out to give her a fatherly squeeze I misjudged how far she'd scrunched against her door. My hand plopped on the padded console like a dead fish and I left it there.

Turning into the entrance, I pulled over and stopped. When I was young, this field had been an orchard and every autumn the farmer sold bags of apples from a roadside table. A sign was taped to a mason jar that read, "Pay here."

When had the stand disappeared like so many other pieces of my past?

Ignoring the teenage frost, I gave her some driving pointers reminding myself to speak in a soft voice and not my usual tone of late. I ended with, "Any questions?"

Winter was about over. Thick, boot-sucking sludge oozed out of the raw ground. There were acres of it, not a single apple tree left to testify.

Finally, Samantha turned to me. "What if I run over something? Like a kitten."

"Christ, drop it!" I snapped, forgetting my promise, "Enough is enough."

I crushed the steering wheel with my grip. I'd hoped this would be a time we could spend together and now some rescued pound mongrel, or whatever it was, had ruined everything. If I'd had a son, he would have made a joke like, "Road kill for dinner, way to go, Dad!"

Luckily, she kept her trap shut.

I said, "It depends," realizing immediately how weak that sounded. On my side of the car the mud looked like it could be sliced into fudge squares. Fudge mud, mud fudge.

"Animals have souls too," she said in an even, adult-sounding voice.

She looked at me and I knew that the big questions about Sin and Redemption, God and Death were all new to her. Long ago I'd given up asking, let alone finding, answers. Not that she'd listen to me, someone too stupid to use an IPod or re-set the car's digital clock.

"They do," she insisted, and added, "For your information, I'm going to be a vegetarian."

I wanted to throw it right back at her high-and-mighty self by asking, 'How about chickens? Don't they have souls? Those barbecued wings sure taste heavenly.' Instead, I took a deep breath reminding myself once again that she was my daughter and not some stranger I didn't particularly like.

"Time to drive," I said.

Her warmth still clung as I settled into the unfamiliar shotgun seat. Adeptly she located the switches and knobs for lights, wipers, turn signal, and so on. After adjusting the mirrors, she turned the key and shifted into drive. Within a few minutes it was obvious that some pimply punk had been giving her lessons while they discussed God and how He loved kittens and puppies the same as, maybe more than, humans.

Beneath the tires, gravel crunched. She white-knuckled the steering wheel but otherwise seemed cool. It got my goat that she could be so smooth with no help from me. It wasn't that long ago that she thought I knew the answers to just about everything.

"Turn here and stop," I said, pointing to the right. She braked smoothly. "Now back up."

Shifting into reverse, she turned to look out the rear window, careful not to touch me with her arm. I couldn't remember the last time we'd hugged. Her other hand gripped the wheel and then she pushed the gas.

"Whoa!" I shouted. Before the word was out of my mouth the car skittered backward off the gravel, wallowing in the muck.

"I thought it was the brake," she said simply, and smoothed her hair with her hand.

"Christ," I wanted to yell, "how about saying, 'Oops sorry,' for a change?" Likely, I'd hear some smart-mouth jab, like, "Why can't we have a car made in this century?"

Stalemated, we sat, our eyes fixed on the bleak horizon.

Crossing my fingers, I gave in. "Put it in drive and s-l-o-w-l-y push the gas." The whine of spinning tires killed any hope of easy escape.

Samantha turned to me with a "now what?" expression.

"I'll get out and push," I said finally. "Just go easy on the gas when I tell you."

She remained steely and silent, and I gave her my hard-eye stare. "Did you hear me?"

She nodded grimly and I slid out of the car into the mud.

It was still frozen a few inches below the surface which explained why we hadn't sunk to the axle. Slipping my way to the rear of the car, I hung on for dear life.

"Okay," I shouted, getting a grip on the bumper. Just then, the music vibrated through the whole car into my arms. No way could she hear me, and I screamed, "You're a pain in the ass!"

This was insane. It wasn't that long ago that we were pals lazily kicking a soccer ball back and forth or going to yard sales looking for dress-up costumes. Now, we could barely spend ten minutes together without getting into it.

Pushing with all I had, I could hear tires spinning and had to turn my head to avoid being smacked in the face with mud golf balls. "Stop, Stop!" I yelled and pounded on the fender until my hand hurt like hell.

Making my way to the front I yanked one foot at a time out of the clinging muck, struggling to keep the other from skiing out from under me. Once I reached Samantha's window, I motioned for her to roll it down then sagged against the door.

"Turn off the goddamn radio," I yelled, but she was already poking the button.

Steamy puffs came out of my slack mouth as I caught my breath. Samantha slumped over the steering wheel. Fed up, I was about to tell her off when she turned my way. Her face clearly said she'd had enough of me too.

Then firmly she said, "I'm going to help that puppy even if I have to walk."

That's it, I said to myself. Then before I could say, "Hit the highway," my feet skated off in opposite directions. My hands slammed loudly against the car roof as I reached to catch hold. Her head snapped back. Maybe she finally got that I was royally pissed.

"Keep it slow and steady," I huffed, attempting to calm my breathing. Then I slip-slided back to the rear of the car, feeling that I'd finally made a point.

Hunkered down, I shouted, "Now!" pushing with everything I had. Mud spurted, the car wagged side-to-side, then crept forward. "Easy!" I yelled, and she eased off the gas but I was just about out of steam.

Unexpectedly, the car took off like a startled rabbit. For a moment I hung in the air, then dove into the muck as if sliding headfirst into second base. Ready to kill, I slithered up onto the gravel primed to scream, "It'll be a cold day in Hell before you get a license!" But the car wasn't idling nearby with Samantha ready to make her plea, "It wasn't my fault!"

What the hell? She'd taken the cross street and had already barreled down the next block. A second later she sped by, her laser eyes fixed on escape.

My mud-caked hand automatically moved into the air as if about to wave goodbye. Good on her word, Samantha headed straight for the county road and took off toward town.

All the angry bones in my body suddenly turned soft as fudge mud. Christ, if I weren't so cheap I'd have a cell phone. But all I could do was hope she was okay.

Momentarily I had the notion of being left behind in this dreary, empty place, slowly sinking out of sight like one of those dinosaurs in a tar pit. No memorial for me, not even a single red milk crate with a shiny "Daddy, I Love You!" balloon tied to it.

Curiously, I couldn't work up an ounce of anger over this and wondered why. Maybe it wasn't exactly Samantha that got me so riled up these days.

With no one around to give a damn, I squished my way to a nearly completed house, the cold seeping under my damp clothes. The wrap-around porch offered some protection from the wind. I gripped the handrail like I was captain of the household and surveyed my sea of sludge. I'd hire a lawn care service so that eventually grass would look like my own emerald ocean.

But I'd never make enough money to pay the utility bills for this pile. Hell, I couldn't even be a decent father when it counted, and that didn't cost a damn cent.

Rain started pattering on the porch roof and it was time to push off, to soldier on, like I'd always done. Then I heard the far-off growl of a car, too faint to know if it was mine. Maybe she couldn't find her way to town or got scared and was coming back?

I scrambled down the steps into the rain and sloppy yard, raising both hands high primed to shout, "Here, I'm here!"

Arms trembling, heart banging like a drum, I stared toward the county road hoping like crazy that Sammy might need me still. For just a little while longer.

The end.

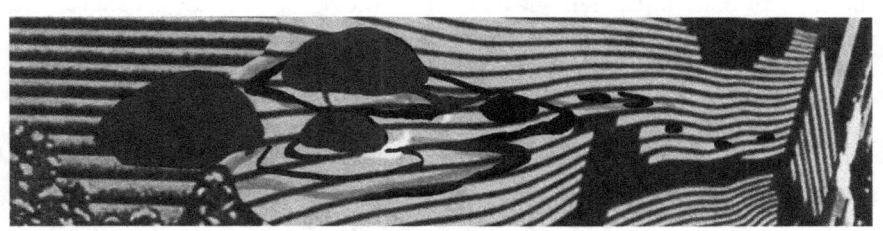

Too Much Dead Time

Howard opened the unexpected package with a New York return address. It came from a lawyer handling the estate of Jo Tay, an uncle of his late wife, Helen. Inside, folded in a letter was a photo of Jo Tay smiling broadly, standing in front of the monument wrongly commemorating his death in 1917. Beneath the letter, nestled among the foam peanuts was a faded leather pouch no bigger than an old-fashioned coin purse. Howard recognized it immediately from his only visit with Jo while doing research on Helen's family tree. Aside from the addition of some of Jo's ashes to the pouch, there were no other details or final instructions.

As he studied the picture, Howard recalled how important the pouch was to Jo. But why, Howard wondered, had something so precious now been entrusted to him?

When the worry about what to do with the pouch bothered him too much, Howard climbed into his car to wander the city that had changed so dramatically since he was a boy. Forlorn musings crowded out other thoughts but finally he was pulled back here, to this cemetery on the east side of Baltimore where he'd first encountered the monument with its eternally wrong story. Perhaps it was time to concede that his research was finally completed, he concluded, and do something else with whatever time he had left.

On the streets around the cemetery, streetlights flickered on and then ramped up to full brightness. Discouraged, he recalled the reason for his first visit. It was just to find a grave, the last piece of a genealogical puzzle, and then his "Helen project" would be finished. She would have ribbed his foolishness. "Why would anyone care about my ancestors?" she'd have said, laughing.

Now here he was again, at the far-western extremity of the cemetery, I-95 Traffic rumbling to the east, skeletal tree branches dark against the Baltimore skyline. Finding a "lost" uncle that even Helen hadn't known about had been an exciting discovery. Jo Tay was little more than a rumor of a young boy's death and the family moving on. That's why Howard had left researching him until last. He didn't want his "Helen project" to be done and have to give in to his children's prodding that he, too, 'move on.'

Three years ago, during their annual family vacation in Ocean City, they'd scattered Helen's ashes at the beach. A vial of sand was all he'd kept as a memento. There was no granite marker where he could leave flowers or touch carved letters, *Helen, Beloved wife of* . . . He could sift beach sand at Ocean City forever and not find a grain of Helen. And now, even his memories of her were slowly washing away as the ebb tide of his life drew near.

A bit of genealogical hearsay had led Howard to this forlorn place in search of Helen's barely known uncle. On what was likely a futile hunt, Howard stood in front of the cemetery gates as his long shadow slanted through the bars aligning with those of the headstones. This could be the culmination of a years' long quest to track down Helen's family history. A hundred to one, maybe a thousand to one, Howard ticked off the odds that Jo Tay was buried there. Gravel covered lanes and burial rows meandered over several acres. Despite the long odds of finding the grave, this was the last genealogical loose end remaining in his search.

The kids kept chiding him to keep busy in retirement, to move on, even encouraging him that he deserved the company if he were to find a girlfriend.

"Sounds interesting," they said, when he talked about days

corresponding with distant relatives and leafing through musty archives. He knew they meant, morbid. Their concern was that their mother had been gone long enough that it was time for him to let go and start living again. Quietly he ignored their advice and kept discovering new branches on the burgeoning family tree.

Howard had often daydreamed about connecting to a known historical figure or an intriguing inventor, some tale of discovery that he could tell over and over at the Senior Center and when the grandkids were old enough to appreciate a good yarn. He'd remind people that Helen wouldn't be forgotten. But so far their collective family histories had turned out to be pretty much ordinary. Still, why hesitate now with the possible finish line in sight, he wondered? Then what?

Finally, old habits prodded him through the cast iron arch framing the cemetery entrance. "Where are the parents?" he'd muttered, blaming teenagers for graffiti defacing the caretaker's cottage.

Hundreds and hundreds of beloved wives, faithful husbands, and innocent children were laid to final rest before him. New to Howard were the round weatherproof disks with a memorial photo that decorated some graves. He thought they looked too much like large campaign buttons, *I Like Ike! JFK for the USA!* But the photos of the dead in the pink of health fascinated him in a weird sort of way.

Nearly brain numb after traversing endless rows of graves, a five-foot high stone monument caught Howard's attention. He moved closer, curious to check out the carved legend, long enough for some grand merchant prince. He slowly read each word, accumulating disbelief. "No," he said aloud and reread the inscription:

ERECTED BY THE FURNESS SHIPPING AND AGENCY
COMPANY OF ROTTERDAM, HOLLAND IN MEMORY
OF THE FOLLOWING MEMBERS OF THE CREW OF THE
STEAMER, RYSBERGEN, WHO LOST
THEIR LIVES BY DROWNING IN THE PATAPSCO RIVER
DURING THE HAILSTORM OF MAY 1ST, 1917
WHEN THE SMALL BOAT IN WHICH THEY WERE
SAILING CAPSIZED AND SUNK

PIETER VELTMAN, 2ND OFFICER OF HARLINGEN, HOLLAND
JAN VAN MERKOM, 2ND ENGINEER OF ROTTERDAM, HOLLAND
CHI PONG, SEAMAN OF HONG KONG, CHINA

Jo Tay! Incredibly, here, of all places was the name he sought. But something couldn't be right, Howard knew immediately. "No way," he argued with the stone. And with good reason. One other name on the monument, Chi Pong, was also familiar to him. Howard knew for a fact that Chi Pong wasn't from China, but was Baltimore born. Chi Pong had lived his entire life in Baltimore and died there barely ten years ago. This he knew without a doubt. After all, Chi Pong was his father-in-law, Helen's father! And, for sure, he was no sailor. His family couldn't even lure him to Ocean City for vacations, "I don't swim," was all he'd say.

Howard circled the monument. Nothing more was written about the men buried there. Fussing at the blatant misinformation, he copied down the inscription. With nothing further to be gleaned, he wandered over to a neighboring grave. A smiling woman beamed from an oversized celluloid button.

"Nice day!" Howard nearly said, responding to her friendly face as if they were neighbors. His children might be right. Perhaps he was spending too much time with the dead. Chuckling to himself, he made his way back to the car happy with this sudden turn, the chance for further research that would keep his project going at least a while longer.

Things got even more interesting. Leaving the details of his sleuthing aside, the results were implausible even to Howard. To his surprise, it turned out that Jo Tay was still alive.

Now thanks to a niece, Jo Tay in his mid-eighties and living in New York, had come to Baltimore for a visit. Literally in the shadow of the monument with his name on it, here was Jo Tay sitting next to Howard on a folding chair in the east Baltimore cemetery. His niece left them with a picnic basket promising to return for a late lunch.

Jo Tay talked about his children, grandchildren, a great grandchild, his late wife, and the garment trade in Manhattan. The mild spring breeze twanged with saltiness from the wide Patapsco River, a commercial shipping route that connected Baltimore harbor to the Atlantic.

"How on Earth did your names get on that?" Howard finally asked, no longer able to contain his curiosity. "What were you doing out on . . ." He looked at the monument. "The *Rysbergen*?"

"We didn't drown," Jo Tay said without irony.

Jo Tay would confess a crazy youthful misadventure that would explain the monument, the niece would return, they'd have a laugh, eat lunch and that would be that. Mystery solved and hopefully he'd have the timeless ending to the story about a boy's resourceful survival—some compelling tale he could embellish at holiday dinners or share as a bedtime story with grandkids. . . . But that was not quite the case. Jo Tay began his account.

"My older brother Chi Pong and I had just started on a trip to China, sent to help an uncle. Wong Apho, a family friend, had brought the news to Father but I was so young I never really knew why we were chosen to go. To earn passage, Wong made arrangements for us to work as cabin boys. Because we were so young and knew nothing about the sea, he joined us to act as guardian. Before we set sail, though, America entered the War." Jo Tay paused and looked to the southwest, scanning the distance, then pointed. "We were ordered to anchor on the Patapsco River and wait for further instructions.

"Shore leave was forbidden so the crew got restless and at each other's throats. When the rumor started that we would sail soon," Jo Tay continued, "the engineer and another officer had to have more liquor. My brother and I were pressed to crew the small sailboat to take them to shore and haul the goods. Since our papers were doctored claiming we were from Hong Kong, they all thought 'we no speakee Englee.' To protect us, Wong Apho begged to go along to translate.

"I was only nine years old and everything happened so fast.

"The engineer was drunk and for no reason started beating my brother. That engineer was big and strong, a mean drunk. His fellow officer was afraid of him and though usually a quiet drunk, this was too much even for him. He shouted at the engineer to stop, but it didn't do any good. If Wong Apho hadn't jumped on his back that devil would have thrown us overboard, and neither of us could swim."

Jo Tay's voice sounded as if he was still talking about his son-in-law's three pizza parlors.

"May I be forgiven," Jo Tay said, "I hid. I heard the scuffling but was too afraid to look until I heard a loud splash. Someone, or all three of them I realized, had gone overboard. I didn't think they could fight in the water so this gave me courage. My brother Chi, bleeding and moaning, had crouched in the prow so he was still in the boat. That meant Wong Apho, the officer and the engineer must be in the water, which meant it must be safe to come out." Jo Tay licked his lips as if

125

contemplating what to say next.

"I killed him," he said simply.

Jo Tay stated it with no more emotion than before and Howard's stunned gaze caused the old man to smile uncomfortably.

"Once I got up the nerve," he continued, "I looked over the side. With a knife clenched between his teeth the brute was kicking his way back toward the boat. Wong Apho was under one arm and the officer under the other, their heads held underwater. As he reached for the gunnel, I picked up a pole—a grappling hook I think—and hit him on the head. Then my breakfast came up and I fell down crying next to Chi."

Howard felt drained and thought a break might be best.

From a distance beyond the cemetery fence came a faint tapping, distracting Jo Tay. He paused and they turned toward the noise. The neighborhood looked rough, lifeless, and Howard guessed that anyone who lived nearby was working or at school. A few more taps drew their attention to a workman on a ladder, too far away to make out what he was doing.

Howard collected his murky thoughts to see if he had it all straight. Though only young boys, Jo Tay and his brother Chi Pong had been sent to China to help an uncle. A close family friend, Wong Apho, made all the arrangements and would serve as escort. The cargo boat hadn't been allowed to sail though because America had just entered World War I. Ordered to wait at anchor, in a drunken foray an engineer had forced the boys and Wong Apho to crew a small boat so he could sail to shore to stock up on booze. After the engineer began to savagely beat Chi Pong, in a scuffle the three men fell overboard—Wong, the engineer and another officer. Chi Pong was badly hurt but safe after collapsing in the bottom of the boat. Jo Tay escaped, too, but in a panic he'd defended himself against the dreaded engineer swimming back to the boat.

"Can I ask . . . ?" Howard tentatively probed.

That moment, Jo Tay smiled. Expecting anything but a smile, Howard forgot his questions.

"I didn't kill them." Jo Tay said. "I killed <u>him</u>," he guffawed, "I didn't kill *them*, I killed *him!*"

The laughing triggered a fit of coughing. Startled, Howard considered, *What had Jo Tay thought all these years?* Had he just this moment come to see it all differently? *That by the time he hit the engineer, Wong Apho and the officer couldn't have been alive?* After a lifetime, had he just realized he was innocent of the death of the two men who had helped save his life?

A pouch flipped from Jo Tay's lap and landed in the cemetery grass. Welcoming an opportunity to stand, Howard reached to pick it up. Not coins as he'd expected, the pouch felt light and warm.

"Medicine?" Howard said.

Jo Tay accepted the pouch shaking his head, *no*.

"Bones," he said. "The dust of Wong Apho's ancestors. Wong always carried them tied around his waist and, when he thought I was sleeping, I would hear him whisper to them." Jo Tay tucked the pouch back in his lap.

"We couldn't leave Wong Apho in the water with the Dutchmen. My brother Chi and I wrestled him into the boat and rowed to shore.

"All this," he nodded, "was pasture. When we neared shore, my brother jumped overboard and ran away. I never heard word from him again.

"By myself, I had no way to bury Wong Apho. After prayer, with a vow to be the next guardian of his ancestors' remains, I removed the leather pouch from his belt. I left him in the boat for the wind and current to decide his final resting place."

"Your parents?" Howard asked. "Did you ever get in touch with them?"

"No, I never did. Like Wong Apho, I never went home again."

Howard would have expected bitterness, but Jo Tay seemed to accept that he had made his own way in the world. Maybe his was a Warrior's Way, Howard thought.

That was some story, one heck of a story, that Howard couldn't resist telling at every lunch counter and family get-together. Invariably someone would get around to the question, "But, why were their names on the monument?"

"Cover up," Howard would say conspiratorially. But it nagged him. Had they ever even bothered to search for the remains of the sailors? Still, he smiled when someone would chime in making up a fanciful version, that the boat had actually been loaded with gold or they were smuggling German spies.

* * *

HEAVY HAIL PELTS CITY, the column in the May 2, 1917 edition of the

Baltimore Sun reported. Howard chided himself, *How on earth did I neglect to check old newspapers?* He'd found the account: ". . . a torrential rainstorm that materialized and was gone in 20 minutes yesterday afternoon." The initial report claimed only a single injury, caused by a runaway horse since there was no wind and hail damage was minimal. But then Howard came to the May 3rd edition:

FIVE SAILORS MISSING
Men Are Believed to Have Been
Lost In Hailstorm While Sailing

Five men had failed to return to the *Rysbergen* from an outing. And in the same area a small bay craft was reported sunk, ". . . her two masts are protruding above the water."

Then he came upon the concluding report, May 6th, 1917:

Bodies of Two Seamen Found
Officers of Dutch Steamer Were
Drowned in Storm

The bodies of a Dutch officer and engineer had been recovered from the water while a drowned "Chinaman" was discovered in a half-submerged boat. Two other "Chinamen" were still missing and presumed drowned.

"Pummeled by hailstones," was given as official cause of death. This finally explained everything, no more loose ends. No mysterious murder had been considered; the authorities had never seen a reason to investigate and anyway who was there to mourn the loss of two 'Chinamen' from Hong Kong?

The kids hit upon a great plan hoping to neatly resolve the issue of the pouch left so long on the dining room table. "Let's rent a house at Ocean City again this summer and scatter Jo Tay's ashes on the beach." Smiling at their concern that he "get closure," Howard gently resisted and continued pondering. He still had remains to guard, except nights were lonely, and his memories of Helen were gradually fading.

The high ground of the cemetery allowed Howard a view of the tall buildings in stark outline, the lovely Indian summer dusk unnoticed. The carved granite story might last forever, never to be corrected.

Discouraged and about to retreat, he suddenly remembered the picture of the woman in front of the nearby headstone. Ah! He had his answer.

In the dim light a week later he found her still smiling from the 'campaign button' photo affixed to the granite. Opening his penknife, Howard cut a square of sod from the softly rounded hump of earth. Digging with the knife and his fingers, he made a neat hole. Pouring the meager contents of the pouch into it, he returned the dirt and tamped the sod back into place.

Rest in peace.

Making his way slowly to a nearby concrete bench he sat, welcoming a chance to gather his thoughts. The night sounds of the city reached his ears and were a comfort, the cacophony of his youth: grinding of transit buses, cars honking, a siren wailing in the distance, radios turned up to catch the game, people laughing, yelling, and mothers hailing, "Time for *dinnerrr!*"

He absorbed these long-ago familiar sounds until he found himself walking the stretch of beach where they'd always gone every August. It was warm and sunny, not a soul in sight. Helen motioned for him to sit in the beach chair beside her. He stretched out, wiggled in until comfortable and then looked at her.

She reached over to brush the sand off his knees.

The brightening sky meant that the *Morning Sun* would be waiting, neatly folded on the porch. His old bones protesting mightily, Howard rose brushing the grit from his pants. Slowly he made his way back to the monument. Smiling, he leaned in to carefully place his offering against the lower ledge beneath the inscription detailing the misfortunes of the *Rysbergen,* then took a step back to admire his handiwork.

It was a celluloid button specially made, with a picture of Jo beaming for the world to see. Encircling the button's outer edge he'd chosen the simple declaration—

"Jo Tay—I did not die!"

End of story, he thought ruefully, dusting off his hands. Nearby humming a tune, apparently content to be visiting with someone on the other side, a woman knelt tending a grave. Howard headed her direction.

Maybe she might care to join him to find a place for a cup of coffee and exchange family histories?

The end.

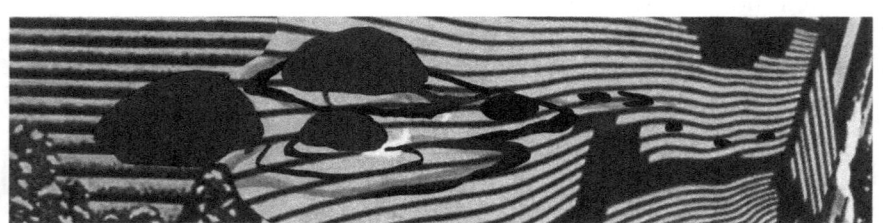

The Price of Love

Dark gray, cold and menacing, the night sky rested heavily like a sagging tent atop each street light along the main drag through town. Bars, gas stations, food joints, and even the normally busy racetrack were emptying, battening down, preparing for the breaking storm. Wind swept greasy burger wrappers into roadside gutters that would soon be filled with oily slush.

Adam and Lisa scurried from the motel to the restaurant. Snow tumbled heavily out of the blackness, pelting them with countless mini snowballs. Quick stepping, they lightly bumped shoulders, holding hands like new lovers. Their footprints all but disappeared in a matter of minutes; just as well, as this night needed to leave no traces behind.

"Isn't this picture perfect?" Adam said, wrapping his arm around Lisa, pulling her closer. For the moment, the drive-thru canopy in front of the hotel shielded them from the cascading flakes.

She laughed. "A night made for love."

"Let's not leave yet. Let's go back upstairs." He nodded vaguely at the rundown, two-story building behind them, nudging, then pushing her towards the stairs they'd just descended. In a second, their playfulness escalated into a friendly tussle.

"Wait!" she protested through gasps of laughter, and gave him a final push that stopped their mock struggle. "You know I need to go. And don't think even *I* could coax any more out of you tonight . . . and I'm good."

"We'll see how good" he said, flinging his arms around her in a tight embrace.

They stood there wrapped in wind, snow, and each other's arms, trading muffled words, nuzzling cheeks and bumping hips.

"Really, I should go." She sounded serious.

"No. Really, you shouldn't." He sounded more serious. "At least a bite first."

In a few moments, she relented, and allowed him to lead her across the parking lot toward the restaurant doorway framed in neon light where they entered arm-in-arm.

Adam was a full head taller and twelve years older than Lisa. At forty-two, even his finely tailored suit and overcoat could not hide a growing paunch. The few gray strands that threaded her black hair only seemed to accentuate her youthful look.

"Let's get the corner booth," she giggled, her mood on the rise again. "We can watch the snow."

He giggled too, filled with the afterglow of their afternoon keeping each other sizzling on such a cold dreary day.

They slipped into the restaurant's deserted dining room, and fitted themselves beside each other onto the same bench seat at a window table. Melting crystals began sliding down Lisa's long hair and when she tossed the loose strands back over each shoulder, a flurry of droplets scattered across the red padded vinyl seat like spilt mercury.

The lovers wiggled close to each other, fitting together like college kids out on a date.

For the moment they acted free and easy, but that wouldn't last once he pulled out of the parking lot and headed for home.

"I'm famished." Her eyes searched for a waitress. Beneath the table, her fingers lightly stroked his inner thigh.

"If you don't stop, I'll give you something sweet right here."

"It's not time for dessert," she laughed, glancing side-to-side to see if anyone could hear. "First, I'm starving and need something big and filling."

Both laughed, no matter how sophomoric the joke.

A waitress appeared before them, a gaunt woman with a large head, stringy hair, and no make-up. Her skin was winter itself, stark white with a blue undertone. A bony hand with large veins running from knuckle to wrist clutched the menus.

"Didn't expect no customers." The voice was masculine and phlegmy, probably from sucking unfiltered cigarettes, its tone flat as an iron skillet. "You either have to be a fool or up to no good to be out tonight. Which are you, mister?"

"Me?" Adam hesitated, "I'm a fool . . . for *love*." He blushed and laughed uneasily.

The waitress looked away from him and stared at Lisa. The look was cutting. "Still have some fish left from the special."

"Give us a menu, okay?" he said sharply, regaining his composure and not missing the slight.

"Suit yourself." She slapped two plastic-covered menus on the table and left.

"Why'd she give you the evil eye?" he said. "You know her?"

"No." She shook her head. A brilliant crimson flooded her neck. "Maybe I look guilty." She smiled, but her eyes were not smiling.

"Fish?" she asked, changing the subject.

"I hate fish."

"Afraid you'll choke on a bone?" she said brightening again. They bumped together and he pinched her thigh.

"You decided?" the waitress appeared again disrupting their playful interplay. She looked clearly disapproving.

"Two burgers for me and one for her," Adam replied. His voice bore the authority it carried in other situations where he was the Alpha dog. "Double order of fries for us to share. And coffee—make sure you bring enough cream." Whatever this subtle skirmish was about, he would win it and get on with his conquest.

The woman snatched the menus from the table, retreating to the kitchen.

"Will you look at that snow?" Lisa said. Her mood had altered a little. "You really should be going."

He ignored that, but said in a lowered voice, "Don't turn around. Just check out the reflection in the window," he whispered. As if he had picked up on the sudden mood change, he sounded uneasy.

They stared at the glass together, pretending to be interested in the falling snow.

"See?" he urged, in a whisper. "Over in the far corner. The guy who's hunched down. Been watching us."

"F.B.I.," she said cupping her hand over her mouth. "On the look-out for expensive out-of-state cars. Part of a money laundering scheme involving the racetrack."

"Really?"

"Better save your imagination for the bedroom," she whispered. Her mood had changed back from wanting him to go to wanting him to stay.

They laughed, the edginess of the moment gone.

Adam draped his arm over the back of the booth, lightly touching her shoulder. Getting back into his groove, he reached up and gently pinched her ear lobe. She closed her eyes as if being lulled to sleep.

Adam shifted, his body tensing, making her head jerk.

"That guy's not watching for cars at the racetrack. They've all left. He's eyeing us."

"Ignore him," Lisa shot back. She was just getting back into the easy mood of the evening. "Don't let him ruin our time. I won't see you again 'til next Friday."

She reached under the table and began massaging his thigh again. In a girlish voice she said, "Come on, be cool."

Again he relaxed. A little. But his tone became businesslike. "It's amazing how much my outlook on life has changed since I met you."

"You sound serious." She sat up. "Your funny bone all worn out?"

The waitress was standing beside them, staring like a wordless judgment. She plunked the plates and coffee cups down, then the little pitcher filled with cream and left without a word.

For several moments they ate and sipped in silence.

"You know I'm crazy about you," he said, as if he needed to convince her. "I just can't get enough."

She laughed, too brightly.

"I'm serious," he nibbled at a limp fry. "My wife can be such a cold bitch."

"And I'm so hot, you're afraid you might burn out?"

Her joke fell flat.

"No. It's just that . . . well. Everything is so complicated."

She leaned closer and began tonguing his ear, her hand moving higher up his thigh.

"Do you think I'm fantastic?" she whispered, her breath heavy with the aroma of coffee.

"The best." He snagged her massaging hand, though, and brought it up to his chest.

"Am I distracting you?"

"It's just that . . . you were right, I better go. Before something else comes up." He hoped the joke would rescue the moment. "Want me to walk you back over to the room?"

"No, you've got a long drive. I'll . . . I'll just kill some time here. It's such a nice place."

Their laughter sounded hollow.

He stood, straightened his tie and put on scarf and overcoat. The boyishness was gone.

"I love you." He leaned down and kissed her.

"I know you do."

She watched him cross the parking lot to his snow-covered Mercedes. Using a gloved hand he swept away just enough snow so he could see from the windshield. Arching his body trying to avoid brushing against the snowy exterior and tightly clutching his coat, he made the task seem somehow distasteful. Finished, he carefully dusted himself off before climbing in and driving away, his empty space erased quickly by the falling snow.

She laughed at her own private joke. *Men like to come . . . and then they go. All of them.*

She turned and looked at the man still seated in the far corner. He rose, crossed the dining room and slid into the bench seat across from her.

"Pervert. Watching all the time," she said, without smiling. "You're afraid I'll skip and then you'll have to get a real job."

"I'm the cameraman, remember? There's no show without me."

"You gotta be kidding."

"You need some new moves," he said, "or he's not gonna keep coming around. Up the ante next time. And get a few hundred more out of him."

"Up *your* ante. I'm the one who has to *be* with him." She shuddered.

He grinned and made several obscene flicks with his tongue.

"You're a pig," but she laughed. "This gig needs to end. Soon."

"String him along for another two weeks," he said, looking outside where the Mercedes had been. "Then we drop the photo album on him and he finds out the true price of love."

The end.

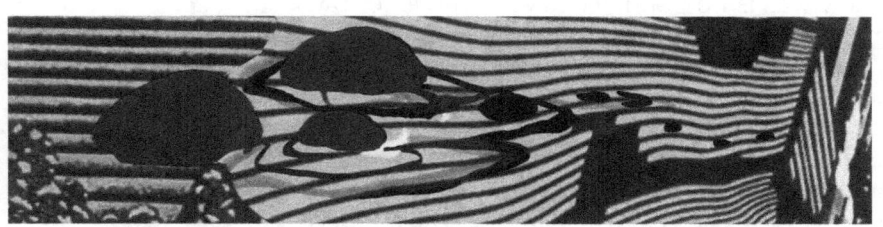

Sweet Water

"Shut up and listen," Daddy said hunching over his plate. Steam from the fried taters fogged his glasses and for a minute he looked silly instead of mean and sad.

"I've worked my butt off to get the money for a new well." He pushed his glasses back up his nose. They'd been mended more than once with black tape from the tool shed. "The head honcho from Modern Drilling was here today. He used fancy government maps and found two likely places to drill."

Daddy pointed to the margarine with his knife. Elwood and me fought to get it.

"Christ Almighty!" he yelled.

We shot back in our seats. Elwood was eleven and I was thirteen and neither of us wanted to cross Daddy.

"Dee, give me the goddamn butter," he said pointing the knife at me.

I passed the yellow plastic tub to him.

"We gotta check them maps because it's cash up front whether we get a dry hole or a gusher."

Behind the angry edge in his voice, I knew, there was fear. We never had enough money for anything.

Daddy ate and Mom fidgeted. In her eyes was even greater fear. She always acted nervous and scared like the coon dog Daddy kept chained in the yard. "Stupid bitch," was what he called both of them whenever he came home drunk. I was never going to be like her, never.

"Y'all know the well Granddaddy dug is about played out. If the new well is no good, we have to move to town."

Sliding back from the table he nodded to Mom. She left and in a moment came back with a funny looking stick.

He held up the 'Y' and said, "This was your Granddaddy's divining rod. When I was a kid, it's what they used to find water. I don't have the knack."

Daddy handed the stick to Elwood. "Give it to your sister."

He wouldn't pass it to me. "I'm just gettin' the hang of it."

I grabbed and he swung away.

"You ain't even holdin' it right. Give her the goddamn stick!"

I peeled it from his fingers. Right away I got goosebumps and could hear rushing, like when I held Granddaddy's big seashell to my ear. I missed him.

"Aw, never mind, give me the goddamn thing." Daddy snatched it back, and I wanted to cry but knew he'd wallop me.

"One of you might have inherited the talent," Daddy said between bites of chicken. He sounded uncertain. Looking at Elwood who didn't have the sense to know you held it by the forked end, he said, "But I don't know if I can chance that."

He looked at me again.

Elwood elbowed me and cupped his hand over his mouth to tell me a secret. I leaned toward him. "Girls only got talent for one thing," he whispered and then snickered. I knew he meant babies. He'd started acting like the older boys. Mostly, I ignored them even though I was curious, too.

Daddy put down the stick and plucked something from underneath the table. "These are marker stakes," he said and put two foot-long wooden stakes on the table. "The man from Modern Drilling hammered them into the ground. I removed 'em. Tomorrow I've got to choose which spot to drill at. If either of you finds one of the spots, we'll be double sure." He stuck a wood matchstick in the corner of his mouth. "There's a prize if you find one of the same holes using the rod. We hit water and the winner gets my American Eagle Collector's Knife."

Elwood whooped.

I thought the knife was more beautiful than any piece of jewelry. The handle was topped with a 16-karat gold eagle's head with real rubies for eyes. Daddy kept it in a walnut case that was lined with white satin. I couldn't believe he'd give it away. If I won, Elwood would never live it down.

"The drilling rig'll be here at daybreak."

We had less than two hours before dark to find the same spots marked by the man from Modern Drilling. I knew the big field like the back of my hand. Granddaddy, Gram and my dog Elvis were buried on the far side over by my old secret hiding place in the bushes. I hadn't been there in a while. Mom told me I was getting too old for such foolishness.

"Go," Daddy yelled and we took off, racing for the rod he'd chucked out into the field with all his might. The winner would get to use it first. Elwood outweighed me by twenty pounds but I was a head taller. My long skinny legs worked like mad and I'd of won until he tripped me.

"Yes! Yes!" he hollered.

I buried my face in the tall grass and knew I'd die if I didn't get that knife. When I stood up, I could see the truck leaving. Like most nights, Daddy was heading for town to have a few beers.

The evening sky gradually changed to black coffee color and seeped through the trees surrounding the big field. A thin layer of mist floated just above the ground while fireflies played tag. Elwood crisscrossed the field like a birddog in pursuit.

For over an hour, I fumed and plotted, watching from my secret hiding place. "Elwood," I called next time he came close. "In here," I parted the branches and waved him in. He puzzled over my invitation and then came in.

"What?"

"Let me have a turn."

"No way."

"I'll let you see under my dress." I knew it was a sin but I was desperate. Besides, brothers and sisters never got married so what could he do besides look?

He licked his lips and pawed the dirt with his foot.

At school, I'd listened to chattering girls primping in front of the bathroom mirror. One thing I'd learned, boys would do anything to get a look under a girl's dress.

"You'll let me see everything?"

"You get a peek."

"Everything."

"Everything you can see in a peek."

"You can use the stick for ten minutes."

"You can see my underwear for that."

"Half an hour?"

"Till dark."

He thought hard, and finally said, "Deal."

"Give me the stick," I said, holding out my hand.

"I get to see first."

"No."

He looked at me with the eyes of a grown man and I wanted to run but my legs had gone all rubbery.

His hand clamped around my forearm. "Drop your drawers."

"No."

He squeezed even harder.

My arm was getting numb. "Let me go."

"Show me or so help me God, I'll hurt you."

"Okay, you just let go."

He did after giving me a hard shake. I thought about getting away somehow but that would end any chance of winning the knife. Letting him look seemed my best hope. Besides, when we were little we'd taken plenty of baths together.

"Back up." I told him sternly as I could.

He took two steps back.

I lifted my dress, hooked my thumb in the elastic band and pulled down for a quick count of three. His eyes never left my private parts even when the elastic snapped back against my tummy like a rubber band and I'd smoothed my dress.

"Give it to me," I held out my hand.

He looked at me wide-eyed and his evil smile scared me even more. "Stupid bitch," he hissed. Gripping the 'Y' with both hands, he split it like a twig and dropped the pieces on the ground. All the way to the house he laughed big "haw, haws."

The fireflies twinkled and stars flicked to life in the still summer night.

The black tape had fixed the rod pretty good. It'd be a miracle if I found one of those holes. At the dinner table I'd been sure I had Granddaddy's gift, but maybe I'd ruined everything by what I'd done.

"Stupid bitch," I repeated the words while racing over the field like Daddy's coon dog. Darkness slowed me down and my arms, about to fall off, shook like crazy. Then the ocean sound filled my head and the rod felt like a lead pipe. Fourth of July fireworks burst behind my eyeballs, the rod telling me this had to be the spot.

Down on my knees, I worked my hands through the tangled grass. "Yes!" I shouted, sticking three fingers into a neat, square hole. "Sweet water," I whispered and started crying.

Jumping up, I gulped several mouthfuls of the clean night air. Headlights came bouncing up the long rutted drive and I figured it must be Daddy. Soon I heard music from the truck radio and would wait until he went in the house. If he wasn't drunk I'd go tell him. The knife would be mine and I'd have it if Elwood ever tried anything again.

The cab light came on when the truck door swung open. Daddy's face was in shadow but somehow I could still see the sad, mean look he showed to the world. He slid out of the cab, bumped the door closed and eased toward the house like he was on ice.

"Shit!" I knew it was bad to say that word but now I'd never claim the knife and hated him even more. If he fell down, busted his head and died, I wouldn't care. Besides, he'd be no help if Elwood tried to grab me again, probably laugh and say, "Boys will be boys." Maybe I should steal one of Daddy's screwdrivers? Then if Elwood ever tried to get funny I could stab him in the eye.

Once the screen door banged, I knew he'd stomp around looking for mother or Elwood to fight with but they'd hide like me until he fell asleep in front of the TV. Knowing I'd be left alone, I got down on one knee and walked my fingers through the grass until I found the sweet spot again. Not forty feet down, I could feel water flowing like a river, enough so that we'd never have to move to town.

"To hell with them all," I said to myself. Using the pointed end of the rod, I scraped together a pile of dirt and packed it in the hole. Then I combed the dirt and grass until I was sure Daddy'd never find this spot again. We'd have to move and I could probably get a job after school and maybe save enough to buy a car when I turned sixteen. Then I could go anyplace I wanted.

A thought went through my head like lightning out of nowhere.

If I just pay attention, inside maybe there's a kind of thing like an invisible divining rod that can guide me. Then all I've got to do is follow where it takes me and I'll find sweet water whenever I need some. This notion felt right and for a long time I'd wonder where that came from.

In the full dark, I felt my way to the far edge of the field and then chucked Granddaddy's broken rod into the spooky woods. It clattered as it found a way through the branches until landing in a new home. I wondered if I could toss myself somewhere and find everything different in the daylight. It sounded good but I'd have to wait until I got my license when I could leave them all behind.

Turning, I looked across the field to the place where I'd grown up. It felt different, like it wasn't mine anymore and I'd need to follow the porch light to guide me. All I wanted to do was get back and wash off the dirt, if there was enough water.

The end.

The Perfect Day

I stamp my feet. I've been waiting out in the cold for half an hour. It's almost ten and the store should open in a few minutes. I've been watching a miniature Christmas world get built. The man inside the department store window has been arranging a little town and the whole countryside. There are tiny buildings, itty-bitty people and even littler cats and dogs. The cotton snow sparkles on the ground, trees, and rooftops. The man is just finishing. He's balancing a tiny Santa and his reindeer on the roof of a little brick house.

Watching this Christmas thing has made the time go by and I can't wait to get inside. I'd gotten out of bed and left early before anyone else so nothing would mess up my day.

"Jeez. True-ly amazing! It's magic." That's what I keep telling myself, to keep from thinking about other things. Like, it's strange how everything can look settled and calm and perfect and still be ready to fall down like a house of cards. I think one accidental bump and the whole scene will fall over, the snow sliding from the roof onto the twinkling evergreen, the tree falling and knocking over the little people building the snowman in the yard. Kind of like when Mom and Dad drink too much and one little thing starts a ruckus with us kids running for cover.

Oh no, here I go all over again, re-playing last night in my head . . . Everything is all messed up. It's getting colder and Mr. Yost is late again. He delivers my bundles of newspapers and Thursday is always heaviest, especially with Thanksgiving next week. With all the holiday advertisements, each paper must weigh a ton. Icy cold air is leaking inside my Keds through the holes in the toes. It's nearly dark outside and I want to be home because today is Dad's birthday. I've got a present for him, one he really needs.

Cold rips though my Sonny's Surplus parka. The salesman told me it was from the Korean War like it was something special. The only thing I know it was cheap and keeps me warm most of the time. A car horn toot-toots like it's meant for me. Mr. Yost climbs out of his station wagon.

"Fall asleep?" He hands me a heavy stack of fat newspapers.

I fight them into my big canvas sack that hangs on my left side from a strap that goes over my shoulder. On heavy days the strap feels like a knife cutting my shoulder. The car door slams and he drives on to the next drop-off point to leave my next backbreaking bundle of papers. My empty stomach tells me to hurry up.

A bike sure would be great right now. Half my time I'm walking— to school, my paper route, everywhere. Can't wait until next year when I'm sixteen and buy a car, if I can save enough.

Finally home I pick over what's left cold on the stove. A couple of boiled potatoes and some meat loaf won't begin to fill me up. I look for dirty cake pans, an opened pack of birthday candles or a knife with licked frosting on it. Nothing. I figured as much.

Tah-dah! I'm here! Finished eating I do a kind of dance like into the dining room, all the while keeping an eye on Dad. You never can tell about his mood. He's alone.

"Happy Birthday," I say in a joking way.

"Thanks," Dad says in a flat voice not turning from the TV.

Now I know his mood. It's pretty much the usual one.

"Where's Mom?" I ask, but already know.

"On the sofa." He nods toward the living room and hands me an empty glass, "How about some more wine?" I hop to it, glad for the excuse to get the surprise ready.

In the kitchen I grab my secret stash of two Hostess cupcakes and tiny candles. It takes some looking to find a clean plate. I put the gift certificate and birthday card under a cupcake and stick a tiny candle in the top of each one. Holding a match to the wicks, I watch little white feathers of flame spring up. Candles lit, I take a deep breath and pick up the plate and the glass of sherry. He might get mad if I make a big deal of this, but I try anyway, backing through the dining room door.

"What the . . . ?" for a second Dad almost smiles. "I told you, nothing."

"But Dad!" I stop him, "I used my money."

He's watching the burning candles. "Go ahead, blow them out and open your present. Pleeeease." I push the plate in front of him.

"Okay," he says finally, half-heartedly blowing out the candles. I can tell he's only doing it because I asked. The excitement I felt a second ago is fading like the thin, gray threads of smoke from the snuffed-out candles.

He sticks his thumb under the flap and tears it open. I know the card by heart. "To a special Father." There's a picture of a handsome man in a suit and tie. In the empty space across from the man I wrote, "Dear Dad, sorry you lost your job. Get something for yourself. LOVE YOU."

I wait. He puts the card on the table and picks up the cupcake, shoving it into his mouth. "Thanks," he says and chews. It's the tone of voice he uses when he says everything. "My feet hurt." "Don't know how these bills are gonna get paid."

"What about your present?" I point to the certificate. I'm looking down as he picks it up. My big toe shows through my ripped tennis shoes.

"Here," he finally says, and shoves it into my hands. "Looks like you could use a new pair of shoes."

I grab the certificate and run upstairs because I hate him and don't want to cry. I lie down on my unmade bed and try to think. There's a hum inside my head that gets louder than an airplane before I figure out what to do. He can go to *hell*. On Saturday I'll go shopping and buy something for myself. I'll show him and have myself a day . . . a perfect day.

"Having fun?" An old-sounding voice comes from a man right behind me. I catch his reflection in the store window ruining the Christmas scene. Oh no, here it is going downhill already. Hey, I'm not doing anything wrong! Why would anyone bug me just for hanging out here in broad daylight in front of this store window? Well, just in time, the store has finally opened.

"You don't have to leave," the man calls as I put my shoulder against the big revolving door. I spin into the lobby and hop the escalator to the second floor.

Grown-ups are trouble, so I take off without looking back.

Must be a hundred degrees in here. I yank off my parka and scoot through Men's Apparel to the shoe department. I know what I'm going to do, because I planned it all out last night. I'm going to take my time shopping and then have a cheeseburger sub with fried onions for lunch. Then hang around until it's time to deliver newspapers.

A sales lady is busy dusting shoes with one of those feather things. I'm going to try on a bunch of different ones. I've just got to make sure the lady gets a look at the certificate so she knows I'm serious.

Florsheim. I think I pronounce it right. From an advertisement I know it's what rich businessmen wear.

"Interested in a wing-tip?" The saleslady asks me, smiling. I smell rose perfume. She looks beautiful but has to be as old as my mother who is at home, probably crashed on the sofa again.

"Let me measure you for size." She leads me to a chair. My knees get shaky, my plan shot to pieces already. Grown-ups.

"Out for a special day?" she asks.

"Uh, kind of," I say, but I'm really scared now and look away. She'll get the store detective. It's no use pretending, I'd never be able to buy a really nice pair of shoes even if I was a grown-up.

"A handsome young man like you would look good in something fashionable and *sporty*. Like . . . a pair of Jacks?" She winks at me and shows all her white teeth through a big, red lipstick smile.

Jack Purcells, I think and get more nervous, if that's possible. Only the coolest guys wear Jack tennis shoes. I've gotta tell the lady this is a mistake.

"I'd say you're a size nine, but better measure." Am I ever glad I put on clean socks without any holes.

"Nine and a half," she says. "I bet you play sports?"

"Uh, no time." I stare at my foot and try to think of what to say next. Her hand is still on my sock. I hope it's not sweaty. "I have a job." I'm afraid to meet her eyes because she'll probably have the same look teachers give me, the questioning one that makes me think they can read my mind.

"Let me go into the back and get a pair of . . ." she starts to say but

I can't go on with this.

"Ma'am," I just about shout and try to stand up but she's in the way.

"I'll only be a minute." She touches my shoulder and I sink as she whirls and is gone.

I'm dead now. My dream about buying exactly what *I* want is about to go down the drain and this sales lady is going to be mad that I wasted her time. Maybe she'll even call the store detective and have me dragged out and booted out to the sidewalk.

"Gimme a goddamn break, just once," I grumble, like my father except really, really quiet. My legs feel like concrete even though I want to grab my own shoes and scram.

"There's the boy with the big dreams."

I jump in my chair. My face is hot and must be as red as a beet. It's the old man from outside, I can tell by the voice.

He's looking down at my tennis shoes with the holes in them.

I sigh and hear my mom's voice in my head. "I can't take much more of this." I know old people from my paper route: they'll talk you to death. I slump and think, in her voice and in my father's, *What's the use? Nothing ever goes right no matter what you do.*

"Why so unhappy?" apparently talking to me, the old man interrupts my thoughts. I sneak a quick look. His pants are baggy and belted high almost to his chest. The shirt's white, but not button down and he has a pair of glasses in the pocket. The coat is like the one my Dad wears, old and faded. Just what I need, another adult hassling me.

"Here we go, young man," the sales lady plops down and starts scattering tissue and stringing laces. "Right foot. Now the left." She hums a tune and has me stand and parade to a mirror and back, then pushes down with her thumb on each shoe. "Plenty of toe room." She studies them some more.

They feel nice, like I'm walking on air, not like I feel in my crappy worn-out Keds. I can't get over how white they are, and the blue stripe across the toe is really boss.

"I think they were made for you," the old man pipes in and the lady agrees. "A young man can walk proud in those."

They go on talking, but I'm not listening. I just want to watch the shoes all I can before I have to give them back. For just one day I'd like to walk the halls of Rock Glen Jr. High and let kids notice me for a change.

"With tax that'll be $14.99." The dream vanishes. I can't talk, but manage to pull out the certificate for $10.00.

I'm in a blur and don't hear right. I have my old shoes back on and the lady hands me the shoebox tied with string containing the brand-new Jacks. The old man says, "Let's go," and the lady says, "Just remember to keep the receipt."

Everything is unreal, and I don't want to do anything to wreck it. So I tuck the shoebox under my arm like a football and follow the old man to the White Coffee Pot next door.

We sit on swivel stools crammed into a long row of old men reading newspapers and smoking. Two waitresses move around behind the counter. The sizzle of bacon, fried potatoes and grilled onions makes my stomach growl.

The shoebox is on the counter. I dream about hanging out in the schoolyard with the coolest guys, hands in my pockets not saying much.

"Here you go." A waitress puts the jelly donut and a large glass of Coke in front of me and a slice of cherry pie and coffee with cream in front of the old man. My stomach feels like the times when Mom or Dad are in one of their moods and there's no way to know what's coming next.

"The food's on me, and you don't have to pay me the five bucks," the old man says and pours sugar into his coffee. "And if you ever decide to talk, call me Edgar."

No way. Like I say, grown-ups are trouble. I take a sideways look at the old man and play with my donut. Powdered sugar coats my fingertips. He looks like any old man I'd see in the apartments where I deliver my papers. They have gross hair sticking out of their ears and nose and his nose is lumpy, to boot.

"But I could use help with some chores today. How about it, big dreamer? Maybe this will give both of us a boost."

All I can think is how hot those apartments are and smelly from the dusty old furniture and Vick's Vapo-Rub. Once you're inside there's no escape. They start telling you about all their aches and pains and the son who never visits anymore and stuff like that.

I shrug an *okay* and think about the shoes. It would be so cool to show up at school in the Jacks. But when I think some more, I remember my baggy pants and hand-me-down shirts, and my hair that sticks out on one side and my chipped front tooth.

"Good. Eat up and we'll walk on over."

Cry'n out loud, why is everything going wrong? But then, I've got nothing better to do until my paper route this afternoon. I'd give anything to get rid of that paper route, and I hate being home so what the heck?

"Now just line up the screw holes and we'll have this back together in no time." Edgar made it sound so simple and it seemed that way with him showing me. Man, we've already put a new plug on a lamp, replaced a cracked piece of glass in the bedroom window, and put a new float in the toilet. He said the problem with this big wooden old-time radio was a loose speaker wire. We had to pull the whole thing apart to get at it. He showed me how to solder the wire back in place. It took me four times to get it right. He didn't seem to mind.

This isn't his place. I could tell that by the way he fumbled with the keys to get in. But he knows his way around and what needs fixing.

I tighten the last screw, and then remember it's almost time to deliver newspapers.

"You have the makings of a fine mechanic." He smiles at me and puts the screwdriver back into the toolbox. "Let me look at my list." He pulls a piece of paper from his shirt pocket. "Let's see," he rubs his bumpy nose. "It's time you get your own project without me watching over your shoulder."

Me? I think. I never do anything right around the house. I'm scared 'cause if I screw-up he won't ask me to help anymore.

Okay, I shrug. I can't bring myself to talk to him even though he's been okay. But you never know with old people because they like to bend your ear with all of their problems. I notice more about him. He's tall with a little stoop to his back. Not much hair on his head, just a thin patch that goes from ear to ear and seems to sprout out of each ear.

"The back-door handle and lock seem a little stiff. It's the old type. A little cleaning and some light oil ought to do the trick. There's a screw on each knob, two holding in the lock and four holding the whole thing together. Got it?"

Jeez, maybe this won't be so bad. I'm always taking things apart. I give him the thumbs-up like an astronaut but I'm actually really nervous. Pretty sure I'll mess up or make things worse.

"You take the toolbox. I've got some stuff to do upstairs."

"I never should have said I could do it," I say to myself. Everything was going good because the lock came right out and was easy to take apart. I must have bumped something though because a spring went flying and parts jumbled all in a pile. I keep trying to remember how it went together but can't get it right.

What's the use? say the voices in my head, and I sigh and give up searching the linoleum floor. I sit at the kitchen table and put my head back against the wall. I think about our car that's always breaking down and the faucet dripping in the kitchen that never gets fixed. I think of all the other things around the house and it seems as if nothing can go right.

Noticing a piece of paper and pen on the table, I lean over to read it. "Dad, hope you have everything fixed by the time I get back!!!! If you get hungry, raid the fridge. REMEMBER tonight is our night out so save your appetite. Love, Emily."

I try to picture Emily doing something here in the kitchen when I spot it. There, on the floor, just in front of the stove is the spring from the lock. I pinch the tiny sucker between my fingers and go back to the jumble of pieces. The parts for the lock are all scrambled, but in my head I can see it now, all together and working perfectly again.

I can fix it, I've just realized.

Edgar twists the handle. "Nice, real nice."

I don't say anything. I want to, but can't. I just keep thinking about my new shoes and remembering over and over that the lock is all back together.

I put something together and it won't come apart.

"Well, I guess we're about square." He tries the knob again. "And it's probably time for you to get home?"

"No, sir." The words came out before I could stop them. Then some more slipped out, "I've got to serve newspapers."

Edgar looks at me and I think he might rag me about finally talking. Instead, he goes on like normal.

"You deliver those on foot? There's an old three-speed English down in the basement of my apartment building. Been there for two years and hasn't moved once. You could probably get it for a few bucks. Maybe even free, if someone moved out and left it behind. Want me to check on it?"

Jeez, that'd be great, I think but the best I can do is give my usual shrug, okay. The old worn-out Keds feel too big and loose on my feet even with the laces extra tight. But there's no way I'm going to wear my new shoes in the rain and mud delivering papers.

"I'm usually at the White Coffee Pot around nine on Saturdays if you want to find me." He holds out his hand to shake and I take it. "Nice working with you," he stops. "Never did get your name."

"Buddy," I mumble.

"Buddy," he repeats.

Home late, again. I'm on the concrete steps of the porch resting the shoebox on my lap. The streetlights will come on any minute now. I huddle, and zip my jacket all the way up. I don't want to hear the usual stuff from inside the house. So far, no crying or angry shouting though.

I take the lid off. The shoes are all nestled in the crinkly white paper like they're sleeping. I think of the tiny manger scene we'll be putting on the mantel soon. Or I will anyway. No one else has done it for the last two Christmases. It won't be anything like the one in the department store window and I start to feel crummy.

Then I think, I can mess with the pieces and move them around, especially the shepherds and the sheep. I can make the scene look any way I want.

What's the use? My mother and father will say, not caring it's Christmas. *Nothing works out. Everything falls apart.*

New sneaker smell mixes with the smoke from burning wood in nearby fireplaces. *At least someone's got the Christmas spirit.* The streetlights flicker like they're waking up, and some fuzzy stars pop out in the night sky. I close my eyes hard. In the darkness behind my eyelids the orange dots whirl and explode. Then I'm watching the day repeat itself, like a movie, sort of. But I can stop it or go backwards to change things around any way I want.

Edgar and the saleslady really liked me, and for no reason, I think. It's like they saw something in me. What it is I don't know or maybe they're just nice people.

I open my eyes to the Christmas lights dancing on bushes and outlining the windows and doorways of the house across the street. I gotta get inside, and I got it all planned out now. I'll hide the shoes and take them back Monday. Dad won't even notice, but I'll sneak the ten dollars into his wallet. I wonder if Edgar was right about the English bike. With the extra five maybe I can get the bike if I have to pay for it, and still have enough left for parts to fix it?

Then I have another thought. *I'll bet I can get it working good.*

The end.

149

Acknowledgements

Finally seeing this collection readied for press has been the culmination of decades of plugging away. To those institutions and individuals who helped nurture my efforts along the way, I wish to express warm thanks.

One of the notable events that provided an impetus year after year was the writing competition sponsored by West Virginia Writers, Inc. Their annual writers' contest reliably offered both carrot and stick for my creative endeavors. First-place prize for a short story in 1991 was one of the earliest recognitions for my writing and, in the years following I went on to garner 17 more awards, included among them first place for three additional stories. I also had stories selected for inclusion in three of their occasional anthologies. Organizations such as these are always sustained by their loyal and persevering volunteers and, to them, I express my gratitude.

Each year since 2007, I have submitted a story to the West Virginia Fiction Contest, which is part of the Appalachian Heritage Festival. This has become an acclaimed and unique curriculum offering at nearby Shepherd University (Shepherdstown, WV). Each fall a celebrated Appalachian writer is brought to campus to serve as writer-in-residence and final judge of the contest winners. Over the years, I have been honored with two second place awards and I've been published in five of their *Anthology of Appalachian Writers*. I received a cherished first-place award for my story, "Carry Me to the River," (which inspired two more stories that ultimately became a trilogy, included within these pages). Dr. Sylvia Shurbutt must be recognized as the indefatigable Presario of this worthy program.

At a juncture when the struggle to lasso my story collection into presentable order had begun to stymie progress, I met upon a chance encounter. One day at my artists' cooperative, while on store duty I started chatting with a customer. This was David Hazard who, I came to discover, is a professional editor and writing coach. He agreed to review and edit my stories, and I thank him for the congenial coffee fueled meetings that prodded both his and my progress along. His involvement boosted my stories to their best advantage and provided the nudge I needed to pull the collection together.

For years I have been a volunteer at Harpers Ferry National Historical Park, and in that capacity, I came to be an unofficial handyman for the downtown park bookstore. Therefore, many a year ago my path first crossed with Cathy Baldau, Executive Director of the non-profit organization (Harpers Ferry Park Association - HFPA) that supports and promotes park activities, including the bookstore. At her behest there have been many a chore or repair I've helped her with and, as Fortune would have it, I have been more than repaid for my labors. Cathy has been an invaluable handyman on my behalf, helping to shape my collection in her capacity as inspired writer, editor and, most crucially, book designer.

It's not an exaggeration to say each finished story has behind it dozens and dozens of drafts. Patiently reading and re-reading each one, to catch typos and inconsistencies, offer critical judgment and helpful suggestions is the long-suffering lot of the devoted editor. Few can claim such a dedicated and skilled editor as my wife, Susanne. Any credit for my writing awards and published stories must be shared equally with her. She gives her stamp of approval for submittal only once a story has been scrubbed and polished and carries the merit of a cohesive and compelling account. If this collection shines, it owes great debt to her contribution.

About the Author

Always curious, taking things apart to see how they work and figuring out how to fix them is one of Jim's earliest memories. This interest eventually led to a career in building maintenance and construction. However, since studying old things has been another lifelong interest, along the way he earned a degree in history and an MA in museum studies.

Jim's diverse output is at turns scholarly and creative. Local historical accounts he has researched and authored have been included in Harpers Ferry National Park Service publications. He has served as a Park Service volunteer for 16 years and in 2006 was named the National Park Service, National Capital Region, Volunteer of the Year.

He wears yet another hat, that of artist. For more than a decade, Jim has amassed bits of discarded wood, metal, and glass that he collects on his daily walks. He transforms these abandoned finds into sculptures available for sale at his artists' co-op (Gateway Gallery, Round Hill, VA). His sculpture, Kool Dudes, was selected for display at Raflo Park (Leesburg, VA) by ArtsPARK and was awarded the 2019 People's Choice Award. Along with three other artists, the Museum of the Shenandoah Valley (Winchester, VA) featured Jim's sculptures in the 2019 exhibit, *Serpents and Circles*.

Perhaps similar to his sculptures, he has upcycled discards and chance finds to compose his short stories. Jim was in his thirties before he began writing fiction and, though he came to it late, he pursued his efforts with the same passion as his other interests. After decades, this collection of award-winning stories has finally come together, at long last ready to share.

Jim is married to his wife/editor, Susanne, of 36 years and they have resided all these years at the same house near Harpers Ferry, WV. Though able to claim only partial credit, yet another proud accomplishment is that their daughters, Emily and Adriane, have each attained their own highly successful family and career.

Jim with "Kool Dudes" at Raflo Park, Leesburg, VA, 2019.

www.ingramcontent.com/pod-product-compliance
Lightning Source LLC
Chambersburg PA
CBHW071944170626
46813CB00005B/1818